SHELTER

PATRICIA H. AUST

LUMINIS BOOKS

Published by Luminis Books
1950 East Greyhound Pass, #18, PMB 280
Carmel, Indiana, 46033, U.S.A.
Copyright © Patricia Aust, 2014

Hardcover: 978-1-935462-99-6
Paperback: 978-1-935462-00-2

Printed in the United States of America

10 9 8 7 6 5 4 3 2 1

Cover design by Rachel Marks

LUMINIS BOOKS

Meaningful Books That Entertain

This book is for the children.

I love spring. Flowers suddenly bloom and our yard has yellow, white, purple and pink everywhere. Nights are cool, days warmer. This yearly promise of new life always makes me feel happy. It promises surprises. I wish that all battered women and their traumatized kids can find some way to enjoy spring. To get out, to try something new or try something again—like get away from their batterers and become who they want to be.

—Patricia H. Aust

In memory of Patricia Aust, a portion of the royalties from the sale of SHELTER will be donated to the women's shelter where she volunteered.

Advance Praise for *Shelter*:

"*Shelter* is a chilling ground-floor view of domestic and dating violence. Must reading for any teen girl who's ever made excuses for her boyfriend's behavior."
—Jane Sutcliffe, author of *John F. Kennedy, Barack Obama, Marian Anderson* and other books from the History Maker Bios Series

"I loved it and really enjoyed reading it!"
—Iris Ruiz, Assistant Director of Interval House Battered Women's Shelter, Hartford, CT

"I love the story—great scenes . . . characters, setting and dialogue."
—Eileen Washburn, YA librarian

"So real and riveting . . . marvelous use of dialogue and understanding of characters."
—Phyllis L. Tildes, author of *Counting on Calico* and *The Garden Wall*

SHELTER

1

SUNDAY AFTERNOON IS good until Dad comes home in Dictator Mode.

It's always the same.

His truck guns up the driveway blaring hard rock so loud the entire neighborhood knows he's home. Three seconds short of smashing the garage door, he stomps on the brake and screeches to a stop with six inches to spare.

By the time he pulls into the garage, my heart is pounding like I've done fifty pushups. Then I have to wait while he checks to make sure everything's exactly where it's supposed to be.

That's because he's assigned every rake, shovel and tool a special spot on the garage wall. Anything with wheels has its own parking space on the floor marked off with black tape. If you use something, you'd better return it to the same place you found it— or else.

Most days, he gives us a list of what we have to do. That way, nobody in our house gets to say, 'Sorry, I forgot' or 'Oops. Didn't know I had to do that.'

Nope. It's all written down for us in his perfect, square handwriting.

No problem when Dad did the lawn work. But when I turned fifteen (a week ago) this became my responsibility.

I'd already had my breakfast wrecked this morning when Dad said, "Miguel, I want you to do the lawn while I'm out. It's a forty-five minute job, max."

Big smile. "Let's see how long it takes you."

Just for that, I'll do it in forty.

I cut the grass like a wolf's nipping at my butt. Keep the lines straight. Clip the edges, sweep the sidewalk. Takes me fifty minutes.

Okay, Dad's still faster, but five minutes over his time is good for my first try. And no fun whatsoever, it's so hot and humid. Before I finish two turns around the back yard, sweat's dribbling down my temples and neck.

Then the allergies kick in. My eyes itch and water and I sneeze pretty much non-stop. But I do the job and do it well. When it's done, I'm beyond hot and tired. I grab my tee. Wipe off my sweaty stomach, face, and neck.

Jump when my cell rings. Hope it's not Dad checking up on me.

Nope. It's Billy, my best friend since fifth grade.

"Whatcha doin'?" he asks.

"The lawn."

"Hey, great day for working outside."

"Ya think?" I push the mower toward the garage. Need lunch and a shower, bad.

"Mom said I could have some kids over for a swim. Joe and Sean are on the way. You interested?"

"Sure! I'll finish up and see ya in twenty minutes."

I put the lawn stuff away and run inside. Guzzle a half-gallon of water and wash my beet-red face. Then I slap together a ham and cheese and go looking for Mom. Find her in the cellar doing laundry.

"Can I go to Billy's for a swim?" I ask, swallowing the last of my sandwich. "His mom said it's alright."

She stops folding clothes and stands still. "I don't know...Dad's not home yet."

"Please, Mom. I did a good job, honest."

Fear and worry ripple across her face. "You know that's not the problem."

No, Dad's the problem. He expects you to wait until he inspects your work before you go off and have fun or something.

Mom grabs her phone off the folding table. "I'll call his cell."

She lets it ring a while. He doesn't answer. Maybe his phone isn't on or maybe he just doesn't feel like talking to Mom. I hold my breath and wait.

Finally, she sighs, slips her phone in her pocket. "Okay, you can go. It's awful hot and you worked a long time. Just make sure you're home by five."

"Thanks, Mom!"

I run up to my room, peel off my wet clothes and throw them at the hamper. Miss by a mile but step over them and grab a towel. Dad won't check our rooms until tonight. I'm outta here.

I jump on my bike and five minutes later I'm cruising into Billy's back yard. The guys are splashing and yelling. I take a running dive smack into the middle of them. They dunk, shove, and half drown me before I can get away.

Best time I've had all week.

A couple hours later, I go home, where Mom's frying plantains. The smell makes me drool.

"Did you have a good time?" Mom asks.

"Oh, yeah. Billy's got a new water game. Where's Ellie? Gotta tell her about it."

My sister loves to swim. She's sixteen—a year older than me, but way smaller. Five-foot-one, maybe a hundred pounds soaking wet.

"She's babysitting, should be home any minute."

"Oh, okay." I check the pot on the back burner. "Hey, chicken with rice." Not one of my favorites. But *tostones*—fried green bananas—are.

Before she can stop me, I grab a couple slices off the plate and chew fast.

Yum. A little sweet. A little crispy. A little greasy. Perfect.

"Thanks, Mom. These are the best."

"Glad you like them, but don't eat any more, okay?"

That's when Dad comes home and roars up the driveway.

My heart pounds. I better have done everything he told me to do or I'm in trouble. I pull out the waterlogged list of chores he gave me this morning.

PUT THE RECYCLE OUT WITH THE GARBAGE.

RETURN OUTDOOR FURNITURE TO DECK AFTER YOU SWEEP.

MOW THE LAWN AND TRIM THE EDGES.

PUT THE LAWNMOWER AWAY RIGHT.

I look at Mom. "I think I did everything he told me to."

She frowns. "I hope so. You know what he's like when he's in a bad mood."

Five minutes later Dad storms into the kitchen. Stares at my spiky, wet head and damp cutoffs. "I see you've been swimming, Mike. Guess you had time for fun, but not for careful work."

His Dictator Mode involves a certain stance—tight ass, eyes narrowed to slits. Muscle pulsing in his clenched jaw.

Hi, Dad. Just once I'd like him to say, "Hi, how's it going?" before he lights into me.

I wait for the verdict.

"You didn't clean up the grass you tracked into the garage or top off the gas tank. You missed the lawn edge left of the front door and you parked the mower a quarter inch over its line! Very sloppy work. You're grounded for three days."

"Sorry," I mumble. *Sorry for not being perfect.*

"You should be sorry! You could have avoided this by waiting for me to inspect so you could fix the job before you took off."

Right, and by then swim time would be over.

But what did I expect anyway? That he'd come home and say, "Wow, good job for your first try!"

Not in my lifetime.

So now I'm in trouble and so is Mom. I shouldn't have pushed her to let me go to Billy's. I should have waited for Dad, missed all the fun.

I stand up straighter. "I'll make it right, Dad."

"You'd better or there will be no more pool this month," he says, each word hard as steel.

I want to yell, *"Why? What's so freakin' horrible here?"* but I'm not suicidal.

I say, "Fine."

"And what are you doing, letting him leave before I checked his work?" Dad asks Mom.

She frowns, turns off the burner. "Miguel worked real hard in this terrible heat. I thought he deserved some fun."

Dad steps close to her side. His voice is soft but his finger punches out every few words an inch from her eye. "First of all, Mercedes, his name is Mike, not Miguel. Second, this is the *third time this week* you've questioned my rules for the kids. I told you they go *nowhere* unless I say they can! What don't you understand about *nowhere?*"

Mom's hands shake as she covers the plantains with aluminum foil. "You weren't home when Miguel—I mean, *Mike* finished working and Billy invited him over. I called your cell, but you didn't answer."

Shit. Don't argue with him, Mom!

Dad leans closer, his voice so soft and mean I don't want to be there. "And your point is?"

Mom shrinks away from him. Says nothing.

"We'll discuss this later, Mercedes." He yanks open the back door. Slams it so hard the table shakes.

Mom jumps, blinks away tears.

My stomach curls into a rock with sharp, gritty edges. There won't be any discussion later. To me, discussion means Dad gives his opinion and Mom gives hers.

Not to Dad. He thinks discussion means he informs Mom how she messed up and he takes it from there. Physically.

Happens all the time. Sometimes he calms down, doesn't hurt her. I hope this is one of those times, since it's my fault he's mad at Mom.

When Dad's like this, it's hard to remember he can be nice sometimes. There are plenty of nights we play soccer or practice my Tae Kwon Do *hyungs,* patterns.

That's when he's more like Billy's dad. You can kid around with him. He's more like a dad than an Army sergeant.

"I'm really sorry, Mom. This is my fault. I shouldn't have gone to Billy's."

She sets the *tostones* and chicken on the table. "Yes, you should have, Miguel. I made the decision. I wanted you to have some fun."

"Dad said to call me Mike," I remind her softly.

She sighs. She and Dad were both born in Puerto Rico but Dad won't speak Spanish. He won't let Mom call him Roberto—his real name, either, and insists we speak English all the time.

So I do. Mom and Ellie do, too—until he leaves. Then they speak nothing but Spanish, like it's a game—The Girls against The Boys.

The Girls have black, curly hair. The Boys have brown, wavy hair. We all have light brown skin and brown eyes except for Dad. His skin's white and his eyes are green.

I asked Mom about that when I was little. Was Dad better than us because he's "lighter"?

"Of course not," she said. "It doesn't matter. We're all Puerto Rican."

Maybe, but it always *feels* to me like he thinks he's better than us, smarter than us. We have to do everything he says, exactly as he says to do it. His way is the only way. Our way is stupid.

I go up to my room and change back into work clothes. My head aches like crazy and all the fun feelings left from Billy's pool are gone like I never went there.

I think Mom's supper is great, but Dad starts out with, "The plantains are overcooked, Mercedes!" Followed by, "Where'd you learn to make chicken and rice—at McDonald's?" And, "Love your earrings, Mercedes! You been hitting Goodwill again?"

She says nothing, so he picks on Ellie. "I don't like that top. It's cut too low. Don't let me see it on you again, you understand? And where'd you find those shorts—the whore store?"

Mom and Ellie stop talking to him, won't even look at him. Are they *trying* to make trouble? You don't ignore Dad.

And then I remember how strange Mom's been acting lately. The minute Dad leaves the house, she runs up to their room, shuts the door, and talks on her phone for a long time.

In fact, the last couple weeks, she and Ellie have both been acting weird. They're always huddling together, talking softly. If I walk into the room, they shut up like I'm the enemy.

They've been pissed at Dad a lot, too, and sometimes they don't even pretend to submit to him. I think they're planning something, but it's a waste. Nothing they do will change Dad, so why try?

I've given up. When he's in a good mood and we're kicking the ball around, we have fun. But this meal is not a good time. In fact, Dad has such a death grip on his fork, I'm waiting for it to bend.

I try distraction. "Dad, did I tell ya Boys' Soccer just got a new assistant coach?"

He ignores me. Asks Ellie, "How's your team doing this week? You'd better not miss a game or they'll lose."

Ellie made Varsity Soccer last year and she's good. I know she likes it when Dad brags about all the goals she scores and she gets bummed if he misses a couple games.

Not tonight, though. No smile. She ignores his compliment. Looks down, picks at her salad.

Dad's face turns red. He's got the tic in his jaw that means, "Watch it!" and he's not eating.

Mom takes a sip of water. Her hands are shaking. She drops them in her lap.

Me, I can't swallow. Dad's about to blow and the tension at the table is turning my brain to sludge.

Dad shoves his plate away and stalks outside. Throws something against the house. It clatters to the deck. Probably a flowerpot.

A sharp stick twists through my stomach, jabbing as it goes.

"Dinner's over," Ellie says and clears the table.

"You got that right." I grab my half-full plate and follow Mom and her to the kitchen.

Ellie and I load the dishwasher. Mom slams pots and drawers. Mutters, "That's it. I've had it."

"Me, too," Ellie says. "He's always making me feel bad, but now I'm a whore? It's gotta stop."

"Right. And you're gonna stop it?" I ask. "How?"

Ellie narrows her eyes. "I guess you'll have to wait and find out."

Now I'm mad. They are definitely planning something but they're acting like I'm on Dad's side. Keeping me out of the loop.

Nobody's on Dad's side. Don't they know that?

An hour later, Mom, Ellie and I are watching a movie on TV. The Girls are sitting close together on the couch. I'm on the floor playing with Moochie, our little dog.

Dad walks in and grabs the remote. "I've seen that piece of crap twice," he says. Changes the channel.

Mom sighs. "Robert, the movie's almost over. Please switch it back."

"No way, I'm watching the game."

Ellie folds her arms against her chest. Raises her chin. "See, Mom? I told you we need two TV's."

Mom nods. "Yeah, one for the girls and one for the boys." She stands up, heads for the foyer.

I give Ellie a "What's going on?" look.

She whispers without moving her lips. "She's sick of him, okay? Sick of everything."

Something in me jumps. I never think of our life that way—that it's so wrong it has to change. I don't see how we can change it. Dad's in charge. Period.

Dad runs after Mom. Grabs her arm before she can start upstairs. "Where do you think you're going, bitch?"

"Away from you," she says. Tries to pull her arm back but Dad won't let go. I know he's squeezing too hard from the look on her face.

Our dog, Moochie starts growling. We got him from Tri-City Rescue last year and he's no bigger than a cat. I pick him up, hold him close. "Shhhhh, quiet, boy. It's okay."

Dad's voice is scary-soft again. "You sure are doing great today, Mercedes. First you ignore my rules and let Mike leave before I get home. Then you try to *justify* disobeying me by saying he did a good job on the lawn when he didn't! And now you're telling me I can't change the channel in my own house? You're telling me you want your own TV?"

Mom yanks her arm away and rubs it. "Sometimes we like different shows than you. What's so bad about that?"

He moves closer. She steps back.

"Not that I have to answer such a stupid question," Dad says, "But here's what I think. If I buy another TV, you and the kids will watch yours in another room, out of sight. Then you'll bitch and moan about me, probably in Spanish. You think I'm gonna stand for that?"

Mom looks him straight in the eye. "Every family I know has more than one TV."

Dad's voice gets louder. "Are you questioning me again, Mercedes? Are you asking me to defend what I spend my money on?"

"It's my money, too. I work full-time." Her voice shakes and she takes another step back.

Bad move. She's trapped against the wall.

Dad stands over her, his face inches from hers. "You're dead wrong, little woman. Your money is *my money,* you got that? I make lots more dough than you, so I decide how it gets spent! I give you an allowance and house money, don't I?"

Ellie pulls the curls in her ponytail out so straight it must hurt. I need to crack my knuckles but don't dare.

"Big deal! You give me an allowance," Mom says, "and you take all the rest!"

"That does it!" Dad yells and punches her in the face. Her head snaps back against the wall with an ugly thud.

My stomach flip-flops and I swallow over and over so I won't throw up.

Moochie shoots out of my arms, barking like crazy. Ellie jumps up and chases him, but he nips Dad's ankle before she can grab him.

Dad whirls around, kicks Moochie like he's a football.

He yelps, flies across the hall. Lands on the rug at the front door. For a minute he lies absolutely still, eyes closed. I can't tell if he's breathing.

11

Taste acid in my mouth. Did Dad kill him? I look at Dad.

His eyes narrow, tell me, "Don't you say one word."

Ellie runs out of the room, head down and madder than I've ever seen her.

Moochie whimpers, lifts his head and starts shaking all over.

Mom stumbles over to him. He's panting and his head is lying sideways on his paws. What if his neck's broken?

"How could you do that, Robert?" Mom cries. "He's so little!"

She presses her hand against the back of her head, looks surprised and checks her fingers. There's blood on them.

"Mom, you're hurt! Your head is bleeding," I say. I want to get a wet compress for her but if I help her, Dad will get mad at me.

He is calmly straightening the rug at the front door. It's a little crooked from Moochie's landing. He pushes it around with his shoe until he's satisfied it's perfectly straight.

Then he looks at Mom. She wipes her fingers on her jeans, opens and closes her mouth a few times. "My head's cut, Robert, but I don't think my jaw is broken. Last time, I nursed myself. Not this time. If I think I have a concussion, I'm going to the hospital."

I can't believe it. Mom is threatening him! If she goes to the hospital looking like she does, they'll call the police. Then the cops will arrest Dad and someone will call the State.

That's why Mom's never gone to the hospital or even said she would before this, not even when Dad broke her finger or dislocated her shoulder. She's afraid they'll take us away and put us in a foster home.

Dad nods like one of those stupid car toys. "Great idea, Mercedes. You know what'll happen if you do that. Think you can pay the mortgage and car insurance with your lousy paycheck?"

She winces, presses her hand to her forehead. Probably has a bad headache like the last time he knocked her into a wall.

Ellie comes back with an icepack. "Mom, put this on your face. I'll take care of Moochie."

"Don't you touch that damn mutt!" Dad yells and shoves Ellie so hard she slams into the corner of the coffee table. She's wearing shorts and I cringe when I hear the thud, watch the long scrape on one side of her knee turn red. Dad has never hurt Ellie before. Our lows just keep getting lower.

Mom jumps between them and yells, "Robert, stop! Stop it! Look what you did to her!"

Dad is standing over Mom like he's the lion and she's the mouse, but he looks at Ellie. Sees blood running down her leg and a bruise forming next to her knee.

His fists uncurl. He drops to the couch, stares at the TV.

Mom helps Ellie up, slips an arm around her waist. "Come on, honey. Let's take care of your leg." They head for the kitchen, Ellie limping, Mom pressing the ice bag on her jaw.

I hear water running in the half bath and Ellie crying.

Can't believe how bad Dad hurt her. Usually, he just yells at us kids if we mess up. Grounds us or tortures us with sermons that go on and on until we feel like turds. But this time he hurt Ellie! Who's next—me?

I sit at the other end of the couch, as far away from him as I can get. I'm dying to run to the kitchen, see if Mom and Ellie are all right.

Moochie lifts his head. He's panting like crazy and his eyes are wild. I want to pick him up, calm him down. Make sure nothing's broken.

Dad leans toward me, taps the top of the couch six inches from my shoulder. "Forget it, Mike, okay? Let's just watch the game."

His voice echoes in my head. "Us men gotta stick together."

Doing what, beating up women?

I don't move. Don't want Dad to notice me or keep talking to me. But if he does, I won't ignore him like Mom and Ellie did at supper because I'm not stupid. When Dad's in Dictator Mode, you shut up, do what he tells you to do. You don't aggravate him over a stupid movie!

On TV, the announcer's going nuts. Someone just hit a grand slam to win the game. Dad doesn't react.

I sneak a look at the biggest fan the Red Sox ever had. He's staring out the front window. Maybe he's thinking about something else, like how he's a bully and a jerk.

Yeah, right.

Mom returns to the living room alone. She's crying, blowing her nose. Still has the ice bag pressed against her jaw.

I hate this. Are there other kids like me? I can't be the only kid in the world whose father thinks he has the right to beat up his family and dog.

My stomach clenches when I realize Ellie's not with Mom. What if she's had it with Dad, too and takes off? I wouldn't blame her but I don't want to be the only kid stuck at home with the Dictator, either. It'll all be on my head—being perfect, pretending to respect him, protecting myself and Mom. It'll be too much. I need my sister.

I hear Master Han's voice in my head. *Respect and obey your parents. Be courteous and honest. Show self-control and indomitable spirit.*

Nice words and he's right. They just don't fit what I have to deal with every day.

Master Han owns my *dojang*—my Tae Kwon Do school. His rank is ninth *dan*—the highest level black belt. He is patient and kind. I like and respect him. But he has no idea what happens in my house.

Then there's Dad, polar opposite of Master Han. Not patient. Not kind. Knows exactly what he's doing and doesn't care how he hurts us in the process.

He frowns when Mom tucks the ice bag under her chin. Watches her lift Moochie's legs one by one.

Grabs the remote and raises the volume on the post-game review. What a guy.

She ignores him. Wipes her eyes and sets the icepack on the floor. "Poor baby," she whispers. Looks the rest of Moochie over. She cares, even if Dad doesn't.

Her jaw has turned red and is swelling up pretty good. She's frowning—her head probably hurts, too. No way is she going to work tomorrow.

I hate Dad for what he did to her, but I don't show it. Don't say a word. He'd probably let me have it if I joined Mom on the floor, asked her if she's all right or could I do anything for her. And I'm not ready to become another one of the wounded around here.

Maybe I'm strange. I'm fifteen, pretty big and strong for my age. Maybe I'm a wuss.

But what should I do to stop Dad from hurting us when he's in Dictator Mode?

Do I pull him off Mom? Call 911 before he grabs me?

How about if I yell, "Ki-hap!" and deck him with my best side kick?

Right.

He's bigger, meaner, stronger, and faster than me. He's a rotten bully and there's no way I can beat him at anything. So I go into Survivor Mode when the fireworks start. Get as far away from him as possible. If I can't get away, I pull back. Turn to stone.

Aim for invisible.

Maybe I'm just a coward.

2

DIEGO: *HEY,* BOOTIFUL *girl. can't wait 2 see u. how u doin?*

Ellie: *not so hot. dad hurt mom and me 2nite.*

Diego: *accident or what?*

Ellie: *no accident. he just felt like it.*

Diego: *cant beleeve it. he s way better than my dad.*

Ellie: *then i pity you. besides youve seen him at my house. u no he can b a jerk.*

Diego: *not last satrday. we had a grate time playin cards. even yor mom.*

Ellie: *only cuz he was behaving 4 a change.*

Diego: *so wot happened. u all rite?*

Ellie: *no and moms so mad i bet she's thinking divorce.*

Diego: *wow. b rite over. take u out.*

Ellie: *cant leave. dad hurt moochie bad 2.*

Diego: *no lie. even the dog. wot happened?*

Ellie: *mom told dad she wanted to keep her paycheck so he punched her. moochie went nuts an dad kicked him. i tried 2 help mooch but dad shoved me. i fell n cut my leg.*

Diego: *that sucks. he must be sory.*

Ellie: *who cares. 2 late 4 sorry.*

Diego: *come on. give him a chance. he s your father.*

Ellie: *he s an animal.*

Diego: *i dont get it. he s always nice to me.*
Ellie: *yeah. he s nice to everyone but us. gotta go. my fone bill 2 big. luv u.*
Diego: *luv u 2. always.*

FLORIE: *GIRLFRIEND. I am soooo bored. lets go 2 the mall.*
　　Ellie: *cant. dont feel good.*
　　Florie: *ok then. how about i come over. make you feel better.*
　　Ellie: *not tonite. i told diego he cant come over so u cant either.*
　　Florie: *u must b crazy. that boy is so fine.*
　　Ellie: *no kiddin. so dont think about going after him.*
　　Florie: *girl. yor my best friend. why would i do that.*
　　Ellie: *i dont think you would but it happens. lets talk tomorrow ok.*
　　Florie: *sure. if i dont die from boredom. ttyl*

BILLY: *HEY. WHAT up.*
　　Miguel: *nothin good.*
　　Billy: *so lets hit the dairy. get somethin good.*
　　Miguel: *cant. moochies hurt.*
　　Billy: *what happened?*
　　Miguel:
　　Billy: *u there.*
　　Miguel: *dad fell over him. we r waiting to hear from the vet.*
　　Billy: *poor little guy. hope he s ok.*
　　Miguel: *me 2. gotta go. ttyl.*

3

TOO MANY FIRSTS tonight. The first time Dad hit Mom on the face where she can't hide it. First time he hurt Ellie or kicked Moochie.

I don't know why I'm so shocked. He's been getting worse, acting meaner all the time. But he always has excuses for hurting us—his high-pressure job, demanding boss, the lousy commute, too many bills. Says he can't even sleep unless we do everything *right*.

From now on, he can keep his freakin' excuses. What he did to Ellie and Mom and Moochie was *wrong*. Period.

Mom must feel the same way because, after she checks out Moochie, she stays on the floor and stares at Dad. I think she's trying to force him to see what he did to her face.

It works. He looks away first. Then he says, "Tell you what, Mercedes. You want to pick your own TV show? Fine! I'll go down to Smokey's and watch the next game with my friends, have a few."

Mom says nothing, keeps staring at him. It's scary. She's not usually bold like this. Tries to put out his fires by placating him.

I sit still, my head spinning, and wait for more trouble.

He stands up and *leaves!*

The minute his truck roars off, Mom grabs her phone, runs outside and sits on the deck. I don't know who she calls, but she talks a long time. After she hangs up, she stares at the back yard even longer.

My gut feels full of ants. This is the worst damage Dad's ever done. She could hide bruises on her body with clothes. What he did to her face no makeup on earth is gonna hide.

Then I realize how mad she is this time. Wonder if she called the police. Maybe she'll get Dad arrested!

Another thing to deal with. Dad's arrest will show up in the paper. The guys will see it. What do I tell them?

Twenty minutes later, Mom is still outside and the kitchen phone rings. I grab it.

"Is Mrs. Castillo there?" Woman's voice. "This is Dr. Somers, the vet."

Mom runs in, grabs the phone. Talks to her in the living room. I sit on the couch and listen.

"Yes," Mom says. "Moochie can stand up but he's limping and wobbly. Something hurts him." She asks a couple questions, listens to the answers. Says, "Okay, thanks," and hangs up.

Ellie walks in and flops down on the couch next to Mom. Her leg has started scabbing over, but is still oozing, and she looks spaced out. Guess she was shocked, too. Dad's been bad before, but not this bad.

"Where were you?" I mouth.

She ignores me, turns to Mom. "What did Dr. Somers say?"

Mom clenches her hands tight in her lap, her lips quivering. "Moochie can have nothing but water until tomorrow. No solid food, no treats. He'll stay in your room tonight like always, Mike, but wake him up a couple times before you fall asleep, okay?"

I nod, not sure why I have to do that.

"Did Dr. Somers think Mooch has a concussion?" Ellie asks.

"He might," Mom says.

Oh. Good job, Dad.

Mom swallows and takes a deep breath. Her voice shakes. "In the morning, if Moochie won't eat or throws up, I have to take him in. He could have internal injuries."

She's crying again. Grabs her cell and goes back outside.

"Love means you are kind to everyone," Master Han always says. "You don't hurt others."

I don't think he's ever had to deal with someone who's cruel just because he can be, because he's stronger. I wish I could talk to Master Han, but he has Sunday classes.

I don't know what I'd say, anyway. It's not easy to admit your father's a monster.

Moochie is still shaking. I pick him up real carefully and carry him and his water bowl up to my room. Ellie follows me, grabs a towel from the upstairs bathroom and makes a little bed for him on the floor.

"What're you doing?" I ask. "He always sleeps with me!"

"Not tonight," she says. "We have to be careful. You might roll on him."

"Oh. Right."

She squats next to Mooch, says, "Ow, ow, ow." Grabs her leg.

There's a big bandage on her knee, but it isn't big enough to cover the ugly bruise.

Pretty soon, Moochie falls asleep. Ellie waits a couple minutes, then gently pats him. He opens his eyes, lifts his head a little. Doesn't lick her hand.

Ellie stands up slowly, holding her leg. Her face is so pale, I change my mind.

I wish Dad had shoved me into the table instead of her.

"I guess Moochie isn't unconscious," she says, "but wake him up once more before you turn out the light, okay? We gotta watch him."

Her hands roll into fists. "If it turns out he's hurt real bad, I'll never talk to Dad again, I swear."

"Me, neither." I look down at our little ball of fur. How could anyone treat him like a football? His round tummy moves in and out faster than usual. I hope he can breathe okay. "What happened to 'Pick on someone your own size'?"

Ellie rolls her eyes. "None of us are Dad's size. I'm afraid Mom will leave him this time."

My stomach goes cold. "She could, now she has an extra set of keys."

"Don't remind me."

Dad used to keep Mom in line after he hurt her by hiding her keys. Not anymore. She had an extra set made. Hides them behind the chicken broth cans. Now she can take off any time she wants.

My stomach turns over. What if she leaves? Do we have to stay in the house with Dad? Or quit day camp and move out with her?

All I can think is, if she stays home tomorrow, I'm staying with her. I'll do the wash, help her cook or clean. Try to make up for what Dad did.

I fall asleep fast but keep waking up, listening for Mom. Finally I give up. Get out of bed and pat Moochie to see if he will wake up okay.

He raises his head with a little whimper. Looks at me and goes back to sleep.

I lie down again but can't relax. If Mom bought extra keys, maybe she found a way to stash some of her allowance, too. Maybe she's saved enough to rent a room or visit my uncle in Chicago.

Everything starts to buzz—my head, ears, muscles. I feel like I'm in Drive but my car won't move. I have to know if she is still in the house. I roll out of bed, creep down the hall and peek in the master bedroom.

It's empty.

She could be downstairs, but I'm afraid to look. If she isn't, then maybe she's gone, and I don't think I want to know that for sure.

Instead, I stand at the top of the stairs and listen.

Hear zip.

At 2 a.m., Dad comes home. This time he doesn't make much noise coming up the driveway. A minute later I hear him say something to Mom in the living room.

She doesn't answer. Or follow him upstairs, but that's okay. At least I know she's home.

Since we were little, Dad's always checked on us before he goes to bed. I turn to the wall, pretend to be asleep.

He walks right past my door.

Hours later I wake up like someone just poked me in the ribs. Only no one's in my room.

I grab my clock and groan. It's 5:10 a.m.!

Then I hear Dad downstairs, doing his "day-after-the-disaster-sweet-talk" thing. "Hey, I'm really, really sorry about yesterday, Mercedes. I didn't mean to hurt you or anyone else. You know how much I love you. It's work, it's making me crazy. All Ron talks about these days is the payroll and how many guys he has to lay off. I can't take the stress. How do we pay the bills if I get laid off?"

Silence.

"Look, I'll make it up to you," Dad says. He's talking fast, sounds nervous.

Wow. Since when did Mom make him nervous? Her face must look really bad.

"We'll go out somewhere nice when you're up to it, okay Mercedes? Just you and me."

Up to it?

Asshole. "Up to it" means, "When your face looks okay." I've heard it before, like when he messed up her arms and thighs in the middle of summer.

He waits for her to answer.

She doesn't.

He says, "If that's how you want it, fine. Remember, I start at a new site today and it's a longer commute—at least an hour each way. I'll call you later and let you know when I'll be home."

His voice is softer than last night. Gee, maybe he's worried he can't fix it this time.

So am I.

The garage door opens and shuts. The truck pulls away and it gets quiet again.

I feel like I just fell back to sleep when Mom wakes me up. I roll over, look at the alarm clock again. *I did just fall asleep!* It's freakin' 5:30 a.m.!

I close my eyes, mumble, "Mom, the bus comes at eight. Let me sleep, okay?"

Mom glances at me in the rearview mirror. "Yes, I think so, too. He ate pretty good this morning and moved around fine. I think he's a little sore, but not too bad."

Her voice trembles. She's holding the wheel in a death grip and I know why. It's just dumb luck Dad didn't kill him.

In five minutes, we pull into Brenda's driveway. She and Mom are best friends. Mom must have called her last night, too. She sets the parking brake and turns around. "I'll take Moochie."

Huh? I twist sideways; hold him out of reach. "No, Mom, he has to come with us!"

Tears roll down her cheeks. "I'm sorry, Miguel. He can't. They don't allow animals at the shelter. Brenda's keeping him for us until we get an apartment."

An apartment? Sounds like she's already planning to move away forever.

"We'll visit Moochie as soon as it's safe."

Safe?

And then I realize—Dad might try to find us. Might watch the schoolyard or Mom's office. And he knows where Brenda lives. That must be what Mom's afraid of—that he'll stake out Brenda's house, wait for us to show up and follow us back to the shelter. We're screwed!

"We can't even keep Moochie?" Ellie asks.

Mom wipes her eyes. "No."

Ellie starts crying, too. "Bastard," she says.

I don't know if she means Dad or whoever makes the rules at the shelter, and I don't ask.

Moochie's looking at me like I can fix this. I lean down and kiss his head. "Sorry, little guy."

If only Mom hadn't bugged Dad yesterday. We'd still be home, still have Moochie. Holding Mooch calms me down a little, but I still think we could have waited 'til Dad came home tonight. That way, we'd cash in on his "nice" days. Life would be okay until the tension built up in him again. Then we could leave before he hurt anyone.

"Ow," Mom says. Sucks in her breath, grabs her jaw. "Ow, ow, ow."

What was I thinking? We didn't leave before he blew this time. We never do.

"I'll take Moochie in, Mom."

"Okay."

We grab some stuff from the trunk and stumble to Brenda's back door. I'm still half asleep but remember to check the street for Dad's truck. Not there. Safe so far.

What a parade we make. I'm carrying Moochie and a bag of picture albums. Next comes Ellie with Moochie's bed and a crate of his food, treats, and toys. Mom's behind her, cradling her jewelry box and a big tan envelope marked "Important Papers—Mercedes C."

This feels like overkill. I know we can't leave Moochie home, but what would Dad do to our birth certificates and stuff like that?

Ten minutes later, Brenda's been sworn to secrecy and we're back in the car. I fall asleep immediately, jolt awake when Mom says, "Kids, heads up, we're almost there!"

I yawn, look outside. Where are we?

My watch says we're forty minutes from Brenda's house, which means forty-five from ours. I'm looking out the window at a much bigger town than mine, maybe a city. There's mostly concrete and blacktop, not much grass.

I've never lived anywhere but our quiet street with its small colonials and ranches. The yards are so narrow you can smell your neighbors cooking burgers in the summer and their snow blower exhaust in the winter. It isn't perfect, but it's home.

And it's gone.

I jump when a police car races by, siren chirping. In two blocks we pass a 7-11-type store with a gas station, a McDonald's, Dunkin Donuts, office buildings, apartment houses, an Asian market, and a line of people boarding a bus.

Which reminds me. The camp bus stops at our street corner in a half hour and we won't be on it. What reason do I give Billy for missing camp today?

I hate this. I already lied to him about Moochie and covered for Dad and now I've gotta lie again.

At a red light, some teens walk by. I duck my head. What if someone recognizes me and next time they see me, they ask, "What were you doing there?" Or, "What happened to your Mom's face?"

Wait a minute. I'm worrying over nothing. What would kids my age, from my town be doing on city streets at seven in the morning?

In one way, it's good we won't be home for a few days. It's always hard for me when Dad hurts Mom and she has to hide her injuries. Lie to her boss and friends.

But this is worse. One look at her face and Ellie's leg and anyone would know something's wrong. They'll pity us, think we're freaks. Maybe even call the cops or the State.

What was Dad thinking?

Mom pulls into a paved driveway. "Is this the shelter?" Ellie asks.

"Yes. It's called House of Hope."

I was expecting something like a motel or apartment house. Instead, I'm looking at a big, old mansion. Bricks and granite. Fence out back. Front porch with fancy wood trim and no furniture.

Also no mailbox and no house number. Not even a sign that says, 'Shelter.'

And *bars* on some of the windows!

Ellie's staring at them, too. "Are the bars to keep us in or strangers out?"

Mom shrugs. "Maybe they need bars."

Oh, that makes me feel better. "Why would a shelter need bars?" I ask.

Mom says nothing, so my imagination takes over. Dad follows Mom here from her job. Parks his truck and waits on the street until she reaches the shelter door. He has the tic in his jaw and red spots on his cheeks. Before she can get inside, he charges up and grabs her...

I've seen what happens next, and I don't want to think about it.

Mom parks opposite a side door. It's green and has a shiny brass lock. Around the lock is a gouged area showing three or four other paint colors.

I shudder. Maybe they do need bars.

Ellie walks around to the trunk but I don't move. Bars on the window? That does it.

I'm not living in a prison. I want to go home.

Mom yanks my door open and sticks her head in. Her jaw is so purple, so swollen. Her eyes are red and her hair's a mess.

I look away, fold my arms against my chest.

30

Mom sighs. "Listen, Miguel, I know you don't want to be here and I don't, either. But we can't stay with Dad anymore." Her tongue twists, makes English sound like Spanish.

"Come on." She steps aside. Waits for me to get out of the car.

The sharp, high-pitched pulse of another siren stabs my nerves. I look around. It's an ambulance this time, weaving through traffic. Joggers sprint past people on the sidewalk. A bus stops across the street. I can smell the diesel all the way over here.

Mom reappears with my backpack and suitcase. Drops them on the ground. "I'm counting, Miguel. One... two..."

When she counts, there's no more chances. You'd better do what she says. Unless you don't mind losing what you love most. For me that would be TV, video games, and Tae Kwon Do.

Especially Tae Kwon Do.

I grab my stuff and follow Ellie to the side door. It's even hotter and more humid in the city than at home. And it's a safe bet the shelter doesn't have a pool.

My sister looks at me like I'm cow shit, even wrinkles her nose. Does her snaky-neck thing at the door. "What's wrong with you besides being fifteen and acting like a baby?"

I get in her face. "What's wrong with you, besides being sixteen and acting like my mother?"

Mom plods up the stairs breathing heavy. "Whew, I'm out of shape." She drops her suitcase and purse on the stoop. Pulls out her phone and punches in a number.

"There's a keypad next to the door," Ellie says.

Mom nods. "Yeah, but I don't have my code yet."

Her code?

31

She already knows the shelter phone number by heart and that you need a code to get in. Maybe the shelter's one of the calls she's been making lately when Dad's out.

She puts her finger to her lips, presses the phone against her ear. "Hi. It's Mercedes Castillo. I'm outside with my kids. Pilar is expecting me."

The lock on the door clicks three, four times. Mom pulls it open and we carry our stuff in.

We're in a foyer painted puke yellow. Mom points to a sign taped inside the door. "Look, kids. This is important." In English and Spanish the sign says, BE SURE THE DOOR SHUTS BEHIND YOU!

I pull it closed while Mom opens another door. We step into a hallway. The air feels cooler. "At least it's air-conditioned," Ellie says.

We follow Mom into a large, crowded office and look around. Two desks, tall file cabinets, four chairs, a refrigerator, and shelves crammed with paper and books.

A big monitor with a screen split into sections sits on each desk. I stare at the fuzzy black and white images that show the driveway, different doors, the back yard, foyer, and like that.

A young woman dressed in jeans and a tank top sits at the desk near the door. She's leafing through a paper file. At the other desk, an older woman talks on the phone.

The young woman looks up. "Hi. I'm Nadia, the day counselor. Sorry, Mercedes. We've got a Hotline emergency. Why don't you drop your things near the elevator and grab some breakfast? I'll come get you as soon as I can."

Mom nods and returns to the hall. Heads straight for a little alcove and drops her stuff in front of it.

I have to ask. "Mom, you been here before?"

She ignores my question. "This is the elevator."

I probably would have missed it since the elevator door was closed and the same color as the wall. There's a small metal plate next to the door, but no buttons for "Up" and "Down." Across from the elevator is a bulletin board covered with papers headed CURFEW HOURS, CHORES, SIGN OUT AND RETURN LOG, and MEETINGS.

We drop our stuff next to Mom's and follow her to a closed door down the hall. Before she opens it, she says, "Just to let you know, later we'll be talking to someone in the office or Pilar, the social worker, and we'll get our room."

Now I really feel like I'm stuck in quicksand and sinking fast. "So we're *staying* here, like *living* here?"

No answer.

That's Mom. If it's bad news, she tries to soft-peddle things. Probably thinks it will keep us calm but it doesn't. I can always think up much worse things than what's actually happening.

Suddenly I remember what she said. "Ellie," I whisper. "Did I hear Mom say 'our room,' as in one room, *singular?*"

Ellie shrugs. We know better than to ask.

Right before we get to the dining room door, I see a pink baby sock, broken crayon, and a plastic truck missing two wheels on the hall floor. Behind the door someone's making cinnamon toast, and I hear music, people talking, a baby crying.

My stomach gurgles. Wish it would stop. Who wants to eat breakfast with strangers?

"You hungry?" Mom asks. She looks as scared as I feel. Smoothes her hair, takes a big breath and says, "Don't worry, you'll get to know the other residents real fast."

Great. I'm officially a shelter "resident" and even here, Mom can read my mind.

4

DIEGO: *ELLIE. WHATS going on? its 845 a.m. an no one s at your house. i was taking u to brekfast 2day. u forget.*

Ellie: *oh sorry. family emergency. omg. i forgot to call my boss 2.*

Diego: *is this cuz of what your dad did yesterday?*

Ellie: *yeah. mom woke us up early. said we had to leave asap.*

Diego: *fine but u shouldnt blow me off like that. i was wurried sick.*

Ellie: *couldnt help it. i was scared dad would come back. we had to pack and get out fast.*

Diego: *r u ok. where r u?*

Ellie: *i m ok. dads at work. cant give u r new address. its not allowed.*

Diego: *dont u trust me?*

Ellie: *sure but all i can say is i m in hawkinstown at a shelter 4 battered women. dont tell anyone. i mean it.*

Diego: *aw rite but i cant beleeve u won't tell me where u r. thats cold.*

Ellie: *sorry. thats how its gotta b.*

Diego:

Ellie: *why r u mad at me? i didnt rite the shelter rules.*

Diego:

Ellie: *if u loved me u would understand. i cant tell you where i am. period.*

Diego:

Ellie: *fine. heres the bird 4 ya. times 2.*

∾   ∾   ∾

BILLY: *HEY. LETS skip camp 2day. take a bus to the lake. maybe liz will be there.*

Miguel: *dont tempt me cuz i cant cut days this week. i m in the talent show. got rehearsals.*

Billy: *oh. okay. how about we do our pig out thing tonite. dairy queen.*

Miguel: *hold on.*

Billy:

Miguel: *had to check with mom. cant do it. got my cousins b day party.*

Billy: *geez. your calendar is way 2 full 4 me. let me know when u have a minute.*

Miguel: *sorry. ttyl.*

5

WELCOME TO THE House of Hope dining room. Four long tables in a row, each with five or six chairs. Big kitchen to the left, behind the breakfast bar. There are piles of plates, bowls, plastic forks and spoons, cups on the bar. Plus coffee maker, toaster, food, juice, and milk.

I'm eating generic cornflakes with 2% milk. They're not that good, but they stopped the gurgling.

At the table behind me, a kid is screeching, "I want my bankie."

I like little kids, but I'm in no mood. My head kills and Mom's face still is so swollen it hurts me to look at it.

Oops. Gotta remember where I am. Mom told us right before we got here that you don't mention the injuries you see, unless the woman brings it up. No violence allowed in the shelter, either. No matter what.

At the next table, three kids and two women are eating my favorite food group—sugar. Fluorescent cereal and frozen waffles with syrup. I guess some moms buy food their kids actually like, but we're not on that planet yet.

I push my bowl away and wish I had a banana. I should be grateful we eat here for free, but it's a shock when even the food is nothing like what you're used to.

Ellie grabs a bagel from the bar. Toasts it, slops peanut butter on heavy and sits down with Mom and me.

"You want half, Miguel?"

"My name is still *Mike,* okay? And no thanks. I'm done eating."

Mom frowns. "She was just being nice."

"Sorry," I mumble.

And I am. What's wrong with me? I hate the way Dad treats us, the way he talks to us. And here I am, being mean to Ellie. I'm acting like him! What's with that?

My stomach lurches and I run to the bathroom.

End of breakfast.

Return, sit down again. A black woman at our table finishes her coffee and moves her chair closer. "Hi. I guess you new. Ain't seen you before. I'm Keesh, lady of leisure. Got laid off this week."

"That's too bad," Mom says. "I'm Mercedes and these are my kids. Ellie's sixteen and Miguel's fifteen."

I try again. "I go by Mike, Keesh. Please call me Mike."

Mom points to her swollen jaw like I haven't spoken. "As you can see, we had a really bad time yesterday. We packed up and came here as soon as my husband left for work this morning."

Keesh nods. "Least you got to pack. Me, I had to go back with the police a couple days later to get our stuff. But I been here two weeks now and things are moving along. My boys, they in day camp so I got me some time to find a job."

She looks at Ellie and me. "Maybe you too old, but my boys go to Big Sky Day Camp now. They like it and it's free."

Ellie almost chokes on her bagel. "We're not too old. Miguel and I go to there every summer 'cause Mom works. I'm an Assistant Counselor this year."

"That's Mike," I repeat, a little louder this time. "I was born in America." It's one of the few things Dad and I agree on.

Ellie rolls her eyes. "Okay, I'll remember that, *Miguel.*"

Great. It's still The Girls against The Boys, even here. Only at home it's not exactly The Girls against The Boys. Mom and Ellie stick together. Me? I'm alone. There's really no such thing as The Boys. Dad only acts like we're a team when it's convenient.

"You need an attitude adjustment," I tell her.

Ellie gives me the "bird" on her eyebrow like a pro.

"Hey," Keesh says. "No nasty hand signals allowed in here."

Ellie turns pink. "Sorry." She finishes her juice, asks, "Do your kids catch the camp bus out front? I need to get to work."

Keesh shakes her head. "No, not out front. Remember, this place ain't on the map for no one but us. You got to catch yo' bus a couple blocks down the street, at the Drop-In Mart. And don't *never, ever* give this address out to nobody."

I shrug. "No prob—I don't even know it."

"But I've got a boyfriend..." Ellie starts.

"Tell him pick you up at the Drop-In Mart down the street," Keesh says.

Ellie nods. "Oh, yeah. I saw that."

"And don't never head back to the shelter until you sure your ride outta sight. And I mean *gone.* You could be followed, know what I'm sayin'?"

Mom sighs. "Remember that, kids. Be careful." She's drinking a tall mug of coffee but not eating.

Ellie's phone rings. She checks caller ID and smiles. "Hi."

A minute later, she's frowning and tugging on her hair. "I told you I couldn't help that. I didn't know we were leaving until I woke up and then it was hurry, hurry, hurry."

She listens some more. Blows out a big, frustrated breath. "Look, Dee. I told you it was an *emergency!* No, I can't tell you where I am. I told you that twice already!"

She looks at Keesh. "I just can't, that's all. Gotta go." Bangs her cell shut, drops it on the chair next to her. Looks out the window. Taps her long nails on the table.

"What's with Diego?" I ask.

Ellie shakes her head. "I don't know. He keeps asking where I am and gets all mad when I won't tell him!" She looks at Keesh, does the snaky-neck thing. "Too bad! He needs to drop it!"

Keesh laughs. "Way to go, girl!"

"Except maybe I should have explained it better—the confidentiality thing," Ellie says. "He doesn't get it."

"Oh, yeah," Keesh says. "He gets it. He just want his way!"

I jump when rock music blasts from the living room behind the dining room. A girl about thirteen is dancing past the doorway with two little boys. They look about three or four, might be twins.

She's pretty cool. Long, curly brown hair, black nails and paper-white skin. She twirls past the two little boys. "Come on, Georgie," she says. "Shake it like you mean it! You got a load in your pants or something?"

Oops. I take back the cool.

A skinny woman whips out of the kitchen. She looks like the girl, only her hair's in a long braid that bounces as she runs by. "Sorry, people," she says. "Jenna! Turn that down or I'll turn it off! Georgie, did you pee yet?"

Keesh shakes her head. "That Georgie—he forget to use the toilet sometime."

Mom smiles, winces, grabs her jaw. "Ow. Ow, ow."

Keesh looks sad. "Yeah, it's hard. I been there. I been purple all over."

Nadia from the office sticks her head in and looks around. Walks over to Mom. "Pilar's here, Mercedes. You ready to talk with her?"

Mom stands up. "Sure. Finish your breakfast kids, and do our dishes, okay? I'll be back in a while."

Ellie's phone vibrates against the chair back. She grabs it. Checks caller ID.

Keesh taps her arm. "Don't give out no address or phone number, okay?"

"I won't."

I lean over Ellie's shoulder and read the text. It's from Diego. He's a year ahead of her—a senior, and they've been going out a while. He's not that tall, but he's cool. Has long black hair pulled into a ponytail, a scar through one eyebrow. Muscles that bulge under his shirt.

A week ago, he came over for supper. He and Dad talked trucks and motorcycles like they're the most important boy toys in the world.

Diego the *Senior* didn't say a word about school or graduation, though.

After ten minutes, Mom said, "Diego, I don't want Ellie riding on a motorcycle with you, helmet or no. Bikes are too dangerous."

Dad's fork paused halfway to his mouth. "Who says you make that decision, Mercedes?"

Here we go. Dad never misses a chance to make Mom look bad. Her face turned red and she looked down. Diego's eyebrows went up and he waited to see what would happen.

I already knew. Mom will clam up, do anything to avoid a fight. That's why her stonewalling Dad this week seemed so weird.

"See that?" Dad asked Diego. "You let women wear pants and they think they're in charge."

Diego laughed out loud and Dad smiled at him like they were best buddies.

Ellie punched Dee in the arm.

He frowned. "What?"

"You can go home now, jerk," she said.

Dad gave Ellie the stare, and she shut up.

I wanted to tell Dad that Mom's entitled to make rules, too, especially about Ellie and me. But I didn't. The last time I took her side, Dad yelled, "Us boys stay together, you understand me, Mike?" And grounded me for a week.

Mom stood up. "I'm done."

Whoa. She was making Dad look bad, leaving the table before he was done eating.

I lost whatever appetite I had. "I've got homework," I said and took my dishes to the kitchen.

Ellie jumped up and grabbed her plate. "Same here. See ya, boyfriend. I wouldn't want to interfere with the important male bonding going on around here."

"That's enough, smart mouth!" Dad yelled.

Ellie rolled her eyes and followed Mom. Diego stayed there, chowing down. Smiling like he won the lottery.

Ellie loaded the dishwasher and talked to Mom fast but quiet. "Just wait 'til I get Dee alone! What's with him, thinking it's funny for Dad to put you down? He acts so stupid when he's around Dad. Why does he do that?"

"Who knows?" Mom said. "Diego seems nice, but you gotta watch out. Some guys put on an act, then they change. They give each other permission to be nasty."

"You mean he's trying to impress Dad?" I asked.

Mom sighed, said nothing.

Ellie frowned. "He'd better not do Dad's thing or he'll be taking a hike."

Guess Diego cleaned up his act before we got to the shelter, though. She looked awful happy to get his text just now.

It's hard to read over her shoulder, so I lean closer, tilt my head. The text says, *"not gonna lie. am totilly shocked u guys left yor dad. i gotta see u 2nite. where do i pick u up? love u. miss you so bad."*

Ellie notices me. Snarls, "Mind your own business, low life!" Blocks the screen with her hand.

Dad has no idea how serious Dee and Ellie are about each other. He thinks they double date with Jorge and Rachel. I bet Mom knows the score, but The Girls keep each other's secrets.

Not The Boys. Dad doesn't tell me his secrets and I don't tell him mine. And I keep The Girls' secrets to myself. Don't need more trouble. Just want things to be peaceful.

As soon as Ellie hangs up, Keesh asks, "Somebody callin' you here already?"

"Yeah, my boyfriend. He knows I hate riding the camp bus so sometimes he drives me to work."

"Girl! He know where you work? That could be a big problem sometime."

"Not with Dee. Could be with Dad, except he works fifty miles away and our busses leave camp the same time he leaves work. We should be okay."

Keesh shakes her head. "I hope you right. To be sure, you and Mike better get off the camp bus a couple stops early for a while. And watch you ain't followed."

Followed?

Ellie's nails tap the table again. She wets her lips. "Does that happen a lot around here?"

"Prob'ly not," Keesh says. "Nobody bad showed up since I come here, but we don't take no chances." She looks at our half-eaten breakfasts. "You done eatin'?"

We nod.

"Okay then, come with me. I'll show ya the routine."

We wipe off the table and load our dishes in the dishwasher.

Keesh points to notices on the cabinet doors. "Be sure you read these rules and check the signup sheet every day for who be making dinner."

"We have chores?" Ellie asks.

"That's right, but you can pick when you do some of them and switch with other girls if you want. That's better than someone giving orders and we jump!"

Ellie smiles. "Yeah. Think of that, Miguel! No stupid lists from Dad anymore!"

"Yeah," I say. *But no Dad, either.*

I don't know why this makes me sad. I hated him yesterday, but he's the only father I have. I hope he's learned a lesson, now that Mom took the big step of living somewhere else. And taking us with her!

Maybe that will shock him enough to change his ways.

And maybe not. He figures he's never wrong, so what's he got to change?

A small woman with long, shiny black hair hurries in carrying a baby girl. "Keesh," she says, "can you hold Sheelpa while I make our food?"

"Sure can."

Ellie smiles at Sheelpa. "What a sweet little baby you are." Sheelpa doesn't smile back.

"She's so serious," Ellie says. "How old is she?"

"She one year old, but tiny like her mom." Keesh bounces Sheelpa on her knee and rubs noses. Sheelpa doesn't smile at her, either.

Okay, my turn. Never met a baby I couldn't get to smile. I creep my fingers softly up her arm. Tap her little nose.

No smile. Eyes big.

I point to the fuzzy toy she's clutching. "Hey, can I see your nice little worm?"

Sheelpa holds it tighter.

Keesh strokes Sheelpa's little arm. "She don't take to new people."

"Oh. Sorry if I scared her."

Keesh shrugs. "It's not your fault. She ain't been here that long. She'll warm up one of dese days, you watch."

The "bankie" boy behind me is quiet now, sitting next to a baby boy in a high chair. The baby is smiling, smearing milk all over the table, throwing Cheerios my way.

Jenna, the dancing girl, and her partners—her two little brothers it turns out, sit down at our table. I don't say *word*. Too busy picking wet cereal off my neck.

Peace is relative.

Jenna's little sister Holly shows up with a boy named Carter who looks about twelve. Ellie sits down next to me and whispers, "He just moved in. Is he rock star handsome or what?"

I admit he has that look—the long, curly hair, the mocking smile, anemic skin. I don't like his smile though. Reminds me of Dad's when he's letting you know how superior he is to you. When he's getting ready to put you down.

"Go for it," I say. Purse my lips and make kissing noises.

Ellie whacks my arm. "Cut it out. I don't need a boyfriend."

I look at the kids all around me and their moms. How will I ever remember so many new names and figure out which kids go with which moms?

I'm freed from that problem when Mom walks in. "Kids, it's your turn to meet with Pilar. Come on, I'll introduce you and then I'm going upstairs to unpack."

So we get the "New Resident Routine." Pilar is the social worker. She talks with Ellie, then me. By the time I leave her office, I'm still hungry, sick of talking, and my head's bulging with rules.

I head for the kitchen to find Mom and Ellie, but it's empty. So's the dining room, except for Jenna's mom and her four kids. The two girls are pasty white like her, and the little boys are light brown. Must have different dads, but who cares. If they're at the shelter, somebody wasn't a good dad.

Jenna's mom puts down her sandwich and says, "Hi, I'm Bev and these are my kids: Jenna, she's fourteen, Holly's eleven. And my twins, Georgie and Roy—they're three."

"Hi. I'm Mike." *And I'm in trouble.* Pilar said kids under eighteen have to be with their mom or a 'designated adult' at all times.

Mom's upstairs, so I'm already breaking a rule. Luckily, Bev doesn't lean on me for being alone.

I throw together two PB&J's, pour myself some milk and sit down at Bev's table. "I thought my mom would be here. Must still be upstairs unpacking."

She smiles. "Probably. Take your time. They bend the rules a little when people are movin' in."

"Thanks. You got an elevator key I could use?"

"No. The elevator's mainly for staff and handicapped people. And folks moving in or out. And..." She sighs. "And for women who can't handle the stairs yet."

I hope she doesn't mean what I think she means.

She stands up. "Come with me a sec." She opens the hall door, then another door that takes you into a wide stairway. "Here's the stairs we use. They go to the bedrooms on the second floor."

"Oh, thanks."

I finish eating, clean up my place and fill a plastic cup with milk. "See ya later."

Bev holds up her hand. "Sorry. You'll have to drink that here."

"Oh yeah, I forgot. No food upstairs."

So many rules to remember. I drink the milk, set the cup in the dishwasher.

"Later," Bev says as I leave. Her kids watch me like I'm dangerous. It feels strange, but I get it. I'm tall, almost a man. How can they be sure I won't hurt them?

The stairwell is made of concrete and echoes so loud that I pound and scuffle. Gotta have a little fun.

On the second landing, I open a door and step into a long hall with rooms on both sides. A couple doors are open so I check them out.

The first room's small. Single bed, crib, dresser, wooden chair. Sheelpa's mother is in there folding clothes. Sheelpa's asleep in the crib, her worm squished under one arm.

The second door turns out to be ours. Mom and Ellie are at the other end of the room, filling the closet.

The room is long and wide. White walls, brown linoleum on the floor. Tall windows on the left-hand wall with fluffy curtains like Ellie's at home. Opposite the windows, two twin beds on the right. Bunk bed after that, and a closet, two bureaus and a desk behind the bunk on the far wall.

I was right. We're all sleeping in the same room.

Wish I'd been wrong. I've always had my own room. Can't imagine sleeping a few feet from Mom and Ellie, listening to 'woman talk' all day, sharing a closet! And no privacy.

Guess I could change in the closet if there's any space left on the floor.

Mom sees me. "How'd your meeting with Pilar go, Miguel?" She drops her slippers in the closet, rubs her shoulder.

I wish she'd call me Mike. Everyone in the neighborhood and at school does.

"It went okay. Pilar's all right, but I'm done talking about Dad and safety plans. And rules."

Mom nods. "Ditto." Hangs up a couple blouses.

"Did Pilar tell you she runs kids' groups on Wednesday night?" Ellie asks. "And they have babysitters to watch the babies and the kids who are waiting for group?"

"Babysitters? Who needs it? We're the oldest kids here. Besides, group's gotta be boring."

"You don't know that, Miguel," Mom says. "Outside moms and kids come to group, too, so there might be some older boys. And Ellie, you could hang with Jenna. She looks about your age."

Ellie shakes her head. "I don't think so. She's a lot younger than me and such a *fashionista*. Did you catch the four-inch heels and tight top? And her little sister dresses just like her!"

Mom frowns and lifts her finger. "Don't judge anyone at the shelter by their clothes. Some people leave home with only what's on their back."

Ellie nods. "Oh yeah, sorry." She sits on the second twin bed. "Okay if I take this one, Mom?"

"Sure, and I'll take the bed near the door. That leaves the bunk bed for you, Miguel. That okay?"

"Sure, fine with me."

Truth? I was hoping I'd get it. That's two beds for the price of one—one on top for sleeping and one below for hanging out.

I open my suitcase on the bottom bunk. "So where do I put my stuff?"

"We're sharing the tall dresser, Miguel," Ellie says. "So you get the short one."

The short one is white with pink butterfly pulls. "Thank you. It's lovely, just lovely."

Ellie smiles. "Maybe you'd rather share your underwear drawer with Mom."

"Sure, if you'd rather stow your clothes under the bed."

She insults me in Spanish. Something about there's macho men and then there's crybabies.

She needs to stop dissing me. It's not right. Ellie and Mom had time to think about leaving home, to get themselves ready. But I didn't get that respect from them. I didn't know a thing. And here I am, just like that, living in one room with The Girls!

I want to yell, run, and throw things, but that's against Shelter rules.

I grab my clothes and shove everything into three narrow drawers. Toss my nasty sneakers in the closet. Leave my phone, Game Boy, comic books and school supplies in my backpack and toss it on the bottom bunk.

Then I remember. "Mom, what if I need privacy?" Not a prob at home with three bedrooms and one and a half baths.

Mom shrugs. "You'll have to get dressed in the bathroom or under the covers."

"Fine, but there's lots of little kids sleeping up here so I hope there's three or four bathrooms on this floor or I won't get one when I need it."

"Whaaa, whaaa," Ellie mocks.

She needs to shut up. Mom frowns, I hit the hall to check things out. "Be right back."

In the hall Jenna's little sister Holly is running back and forth between two doors with unisex bathroom signs. She stops at one, hammers on it. Yells, "Hurry up, I gotta go!"

Someone inside yells back, "Sorry! Try the bathroom downstairs!"

Wait. This can't be right. Are these the only two bathrooms up here?

Holly runs to the other door and pounds on it. "Let me in or you're cleaning up the mess!"

She's stumbling around on high-heeled platform sandals. Her shirt's way too long and her jeans are high-water. They did leave in a hurry.

I walk around. Find six bedrooms, two bathrooms only and a small room with a washer and dryer.

That works out to one bathroom for maybe five, six women and all their kids! Who knew I was living in a palace before I came here?

Holly stamps her foot, yells, "Come *on!*" Notices me and turns red.

One bathroom door flies open and a boy hurries out.

She yells, "About time, loser!" Slams the bathroom door so loud a woman sticks her head into the hall and asks, "What's going on, Dennie?"

He shrugs. "Bathroom emergency."

He doesn't even look mad. No way could I be so cool about all this.

Think about it. What happens when all these people need to get to work, school, or bed at the same time? How about when they have to take a shower or they're sick?

When I return, Mom reads my mind. "Yes, Miguel. It might be tough to get a bathroom sometimes."

"Ya think?" I cram my suitcase into the closet and shut the folding door. The floor is completely covered with our stuff. I won't be changing in there.

"You need to drop the attitude," Mom says, *"Now.* We're here. Deal with it."

"I can't. This place is crummy. Why didn't we just stay home? Dad's already calmed down."

Mom shakes her head. "You sure have a short memory."

Ellie stands up. Looks me up and down like I'm an alien.

I wait for her put-down, her snaky-neck thing while she tells me off.

But no. She moves closer, talks so soft and hard she sounds like Dad when he's furious. "I get it, Miguel. If Mom and I had just kept taking Dad's abuse, we could have stayed in our happy home for *years*. You're right. We were crazy to leave such a paradise."

She leans in. "Did you like living with Hitler that much, asshole?"

"No, but I like my friends and school and Tae Kwon Do!"

"Yeah? Well, what about me? I was Varsity Soccer, remember? Our new school might not even have girls' soccer!"

New school? Great. There's something else I hadn't even thought about. While Ellie and Mom were working things out, making all kinds of decisions, I had no idea what was going to happen. And neither did Dad.

"What about Dad?" I ask. "He'll come home tonight and we'll be gone. He won't even know where we are!"

"Aw, the poor guy," Ellie says. "And he won't have anyone to beat up on, either, will he?"

Mom stands up. "Enough you two, stop fighting! We need to talk with Pilar."

Ellie's mouth drops. "No, we don't, Mom. *Miguel* needs to talk to her. You and I know who the bad guy is! The bad guy is *Dad,* and he doesn't deserve to know where we are!"

"That's not the point! He's our dad!"

Ellie looks at the ceiling, shakes her head. Spits out every word like a slap. "Sooooo what! Every day he gets less like Dad and more like the *Gestapo*. Why should we worry about him after what he did to us?"

She folds her arms, looks at me like I'm dog shit. "But hey, nothing happened to you yesterday, did it? Was that because you sat around and kissed Dad's butt?"

Her words cut hard because they're true. I'm ashamed I didn't jump up and help Mom like Ellie did. "Okay, you're right, Ellie. I'm no hero, but I still don't want to live in this dump! What's so freakin' great about it anyway?"

"It's safe, that's what! No one's going to hurt us and you have Mom to thank for that. She knew what to do when Dad lost it, didn't she?"

And just like that, I run through what Mom and Ellie did yesterday. Pushing Dad's buttons, showing their resentment, openly stonewalling him.

They wanted a good reason to leave! They planned it! And there I was—baby Miguel, all terrified that Mom would leave Ellie and me with Dad and take off, when that wasn't going to happen. What a dope I was, and it's their fault for not telling me!

I glare at Mom. "Yeah, now I think about it, you both knew *exactly* what to do! Too bad you didn't let me in on your plans."

Mom sighs. "It wasn't a set plan. More like being prepared for the worst. And I admit, I was afraid to tell you what I wanted to do. I wasn't sure how you'd take it or how you'd react."

Which shows how disconnected I was from everyone in my house. Too disconnected for The Girls to trust me and too alone for Dad to ask me if I thought anything was going on.

"Thanks for your trust, Mom. Thanks a lot."

She slumps onto the desk chair behind my bunk, covers her face. "I'm sorry. Maybe I did the wrong thing. I don't know what to do anymore. I can't think straight." Her shoulders shake.

"You asshole," Ellie whispers.

I go from charged to drained. She's right. I'm no better than Dad. I'm the one who made Mom cry this time.

I sit down on the desk side of the bottom bunk and face Mom. "I'm sorry, but lately you and Ellie have been shutting me out. Making me nervous by breaking Dad's rules."

Mom frowns. "What rules?"

"You know, like not speaking Spanish and calling me Miguel. Not answering him when he talks to you."

"Who cares about those rules, *estupido?*" Ellie yells. "When Dad's not around, we do our thing. Why should we follow his rules? They're crap! Spanish is *our language.* And we don't have to answer someone who is putting us down, who's hateful. Don't you get it?"

"But Dad has the power. Don't you get that?"

"Chauvinist! You want to keep us down, just like Dad!"

"He keeps me down, too, or did you forget that?"

Mom stands up and wipes her eyes. "Stop yelling! We're living with lots of other people now. I don't want you upsetting them."

I grip the bed frame. "No? Well I'm upset, too."

"Look, I'm sorry," Mom says. "I did what I thought would keep us safe."

"Right. You were sure I'd tell Dad you wanted to leave, only I never tell him what you and Ellie do or say when he's gone!"

Anger swells up in me fast as a punch, makes me forget where I'm sitting. I jump up and smash my head on the top bunk railing. My forehead immediately morphs into a lemon.

"Ow," I say and grab my head.

Ellie giggles, covers her mouth when I turn around.

I run to her bed, lean close enough so she scoots back against the headboard. "Did I laugh when Dad hurt you yesterday?"

Her smile disappears. "No, sorry."

"And don't tell me how great Mom is, okay? She brought us to this dump and left our dog with Brenda."

Ellie's back to ice cold, low voice. "You're mad at Mom? She's the bad guy? Fine, then go back and live with Dad, *mierda!* And take Moochie with you so he can kill him this time!"

"Ooooooo. Little tough girl with tough curses!"

Ellie nods. "Yup, and you'd better get used to it, Miguel. I can say what I want, and think what I want and *do* what I want because Dad isn't here to stomp on me! I'd rather be safe, even without Moochie, than live with a control freak like him!"

Mom mutters, "Ditto."

Something in me turns red hot. The Girls are back and they're still hard case allies!

And I'm still alone.

"What about what I want?" I yell. I grab my football and throw it at Ellie as hard as I can.

She ducks. It thumps off the wall an inch from her head and bounces sideways. I try to grab it, but it flies past and heads straight for my lower bunk. Mom whacks it to the floor.

"Sorry, Mom! I didn't mean it!"

Ellie nods her head. "Dad never means it, either."

My stomach shrivels. What just happened? Am I like Dad?

Mom picks up the ball. "There's no violence allowed here, Miguel! I'm holding onto this until you can remember that."

She stands up, moves toward me. Stays off to one side like she does when Dad's temper blows.

I take a big breath. "Mom, I'm sorry, but please give me my ball, okay? It's the only one I brought with me! Please!"

She shakes her head. "No, Miguel. This ball is mine until you calm down."

"You're just punishing me because I'm a boy!"

"No, I'm taking away your weapon of choice. You almost hit Ellie with this ball!"

"But I *didn't*, did I?"

I whip around, kick Ellie's bed frame. Her mattress moves a foot off center.

She jumps up. "Stop acting like Dad, asshole! Or was that one of your great Tae Kwon Do kicks?"

I lunge for her. Mom blocks my way. "Stop and think, Miguel. Think *hard.*" Her voice is strong and holds a threat. She's not scared of me.

I stand there, breathing hard, mad as hell, and dying to do something stupid. If I do, though, I could get kicked out of the shelter. Maybe all of us could. And then where do we go—*home?*

No thanks. I'm not ready for Dad's retribution. But I'm not ready to kiss Mom's butt, either.

"You're the ones who need to think!" I yell. "You treat me like an outsider, make huge plans without telling me, and then you don't get why I'm so mad at you. No wonder Dad loses it! You're so stupid!"

Mom shakes her head. "What's going on, Miguel? You never talked like this before!"

"No, but I never had to live in the same room as the two of you, either!"

"Idiot!" Ellie yells.

I see red. Punch the wall. Charge into the hall and down the stairs. Whip around the banister at the bottom and head for the outside door.

Stop dead when I see the exit sign over it.

Exit—*leave.*

Leave a safe house.

My heart's pounding so hard I can't breathe. What's happening to me?

At home I was the nice guy. Helped Mom and Ellie when Dad ruined their plans. Now he's out of the picture and I'm acting just like him! Maybe I always had his temper but kept it clamped down so he wouldn't get mad at me.

I stumble back to the stairs and sit down. My knuckles hurt and lunch is crawling up my throat. Just now, I could have messed up Ellie's face with the football as bad as Dad messed up Mom's with his fist.

I have no idea why I lost it like that. I hate what Dad does when he's mad. I don't want to be like him.

I'm not, am I?

I don't need to get respect with force, do I?

Shelter life taps on my shoulder. I smell supper cooking, hear kids shrieking in the dining room. Moms talking, a TV show.

I close my eyes. Wait for my heart to slow down, my stomach to stop churning.

What was with the caveman act? Where did I think I was going when I ran down here?

The living room, maybe?

The office?

Home?

The *street?*

6

DIEGO: *HEY. SORRY i hassled u yesterday. i was messed up. mom kicked dad out. changed r fone 2 unlisted.*

Ellie: *how come?*

Diego: *long and short he drinks 2 much. cant keep a job.*

Ellie: *she mite change her mind. my mom always used to.*

Diego: *dont think so. she is 2 mad and i am so down. need u so bad. lets go out tonite. cheer each other up.*

Ellie: *i cant. i m exhausted and miguels acting crazy. mad he has to live here. mad at us.*

Diego: *i could lean on him.*

Ellie: *no need. he will calm down. gotta go. fone bill due an i m almost broke.*

Diego: *i keep tellin u. let me pay 4 it. i will get u unlimited so we can talk and text all we want.*

Ellie: *i dunno. have 2 think about it.*

Diego:

Ellie: *u there.*

Diego:

7

THANKS TO MY Dad-type behavior Mom grounded me for two days. I deserved it, but it's not happening again. I was stuck in the living room the whole time watching lame movies, which killed me. I need to go outside when the shelter gets to me. Need to run, yell, punch the air, shoot hoops. *Move.*

What I found out sitting around downstairs for two days is what I don't like about the House of Hope: there's no "half way" around here. It's too quiet or it's too noisy. You feel lonely or wish people would go away.

This morning, though, I woke up early, felt okay. Looked around the room. Ellie was already dressed and perched on the desk. Texting like mad. Mom was sitting up in bed, reading a small white book.

I got dressed under the covers, made my bed, and headed for the door.

"Hold on," Mom says. "I need to talk to you both."

Ellie raises a finger. "One sec, okay? Gotta tell my boss I'll be out a couple more days." A minute later, she flips her phone shut. "Okay, shoot."

Mom takes a deep breath and holds up the book she was reading. "See this? It's about our state's family violence laws. I've been reading it off and on since we got here."

She blinks hard. "You know I'm worried Dad will make trouble for me at work or try to pick you kids up at camp, right?" She closes her eyes, sighs. "So this morning I'm meeting with Marsha, a family violence advocate. She'll help me get a temporary restraining order from the court."

"What's that?" Ellie says and finger-combs her curls like they're on fire.

Mom stuffs the book in her purse. "It's a paper signed by a judge that says Dad can't abuse us or even come near us for two weeks."

"And then what?"

Mom shrugs. "I go back to court for a longer term order, I think. I'm not sure. I'm taking this one step at a time."

The bruise on her jaw is fading to green and yellow. I hope that doesn't mean her evidence against Dad is fading, too. That he won't go to jail.

Dad in jail!

Yikes! I can't believe I'm even thinking about it. I don't know anyone whose father's in jail. What if the guys find out? Will they rank on us, tell everybody?

My voice squeaks. "Did you get Dad arrested?"

Mom frowns. "No, but he'll be at court when we both go for custody of you kids and I'm not looking forward to seeing him there."

"But you've already got custody of us. We're living with you," I say. "Why bother?"

"Because I don't have legal custody. Dad can snatch you anytime and nothing will happen to him."

"Wouldn't it be easier to give him another chance?" I ask. "He's gotta be sorry."

Ellie rolls her eyes. "He's always sorry, *estupido*—until the next time!"

Mom nods. "Miguel, I gave him too many chances already and now he's hurt Ellie and Moochie. You could be next. I don't want him around me or you kids, period."

"Fine with me," Ellie says. "I don't want to visit him. He'll spend the whole time trying to find out where we're living."

"That's bull," I say. "You don't know what he'll do. He's gotta be sorry now we're gone. He might change his ways."

Mom shakes her head. "I don't think so, Miguel. He's had plenty of chances to do that. I refuse to deal with him anymore. I'm *done.*"

"But what about Tae Kwon Do? Dad's the one who always takes me to my *dojang* and watches practices and promotion tests."

Ellie's neck does its snaky thing. "Right, let's be sure not to miss any Tae Kwon Do lessons so we can have *two* guys in the house who punch and kick real good."

"I never punched or kicked you!"

"No, but you almost clocked me with your football!"

I hear my karate teacher's gentle, firm voice in my head. *"Students, never forget: Tae Kwon Do is about self-control, not aggression."*

I'm ashamed. Master Han would never do what I did to Ellie yesterday. He would never say what I said to Mom. "You're right, Ellie. I'm sorry. I won't do that again, ever."

"Hmmm, lemme think," Ellie says. "How many times has Dad made promises like that?"

"That's enough," Mom says and opens our door. "Come on. Time for breakfast. I'm meeting with Marsha in an hour."

I follow them downstairs but don't feel very hungry anymore. I'm betting that's *it* for my Tae Kwon Do lessons with Master Han and it's because of Dad. Mom's probably afraid he'll show up at the *dojang* and follow us back to the shelter. And she's probably right.

All I know is, I don't do that great at school. I can't draw, sing, or play an instrument. But I am *really good* at Tae Kwon Do.

I work hard perfecting my *hyungs,* patterns. Practice sparring and breaking with Dad all the time. And I get promoted fast, too. I'm only two belts from first *dan*—first level black belt!

"Mom, I don't have to quit Tae Kwon Do, do I?"

No answer, of course.

At breakfast, Bev agrees to "watch" us while Mom meets with the court advocate. Like we need a babysitter! Mom has worked for years. We *always* go home to an empty house after school and camp! And we don't get in trouble. The shelter should cut us some slack.

Downstairs, Rock Star Carter's mom, Audrey is making breakfast. Her egg sandwiches smell good and look greasy—just the way I like them. But when she offers me one I say, "No thanks." They remind me of home and I can't deal with it today.

"Give me two, okay Mom?" Carter asks. Drops a big smile on her and she eats it up.

"Sure. You want one, Crosby?" she asks his little brother.

He shakes his head. "No, thanks. The cereal's good."

As soon as their mom leaves, Carter checks to see who's watching. Finds out I'm the only one and tips over his little brother's juice so it spills on his pants. The *front* of his pants.

Crosby looks about seven years old, but he drops his fists on the table, squeezes his eyes into a narrow line. "Just wait," he threatens softly.

Carter shakes his head. "Blaming me again? You are sooo clumsy, Crosby."

"Jerk!" Crosby says and runs upstairs to change. Hope no one hassles him for going alone.

Carter hurries to the kitchen and asks Audrey for a wet towel to "clean up Crosby's spill."

She shakes her head. "That boy! I never seen anyone as sloppy as him."

Carter comes back laughing and makes a show of wiping up the mess real carefully like he wants Mr. Clean's job.

"Whadda guy," I say sarcastically. "He actually cleans up his own messes."

"Shut up," Carter says real low.

"Why? You plan to spill my juice, too?" I say a lot louder.

He sits down, checks where his mother is. Doesn't see her. "Cut me a break, okay? It's so boring around here. I'm just having fun."

"Fun? You mean like the kind of 'fun' the nice guys we lived with used? 'Fun' like the games that put us in here?"

Carter shrugs, looks down.

I wonder what kind of guy he and Crosby and his mom left, since plenty of the stories I've heard here sound a lot like ours. Control is the big thing with the men we've left. Control, power, or else—just like Dad.

I toast a bagel and top it with generic jam. Eat it. Find out I'm hungry. Make another one and drink my juice. Mom and Ellie sit down at the table, have cheerios with milk. Drink big mugs of coffee.

When Carter's brother comes back, I pour him some more juice and make him toast under the broiler because the toaster's busy.

We sit down across from Carter who looks at me, then away.

"If you do that to your brother again," I say, "I'll let your mom in on your nasty game, okay?"

Carter frowns, says, "Sorry, Crosby."

Crosby looks surprised. "That's okay."

For the next two hours, Ellie and I play Rummy on the living room floor. She beats me a zillion times while Bev makes calls about jobs in the paper.

When Mom gets back from meeting with Marsha, she looks tired but more relaxed. "Hey, anybody want tomato soup and grilled cheese for lunch?" she asks.

"Yes! American comfort food," I say and beat her to the kitchen.

I pour our milk, get out spoons, bowls and paper plates while Mom makes the sandwiches.

Ellie asks non-stop questions about court and the restraining order. Mom dribbles out partial answers, no answers, and shrugs.

That gets old real fast. "Mom, we're not little kids and we're all in this together," I say. "Come on, give."

She looks surprised, then nods. "You're right but I need time to think first, okay? I'll tell you more later."

After lunch, up in the room, we learn one thing fast. Getting a restraining order means paperwork. And plenty of it.

Mom sits at the desk, pulls out the court forms. Writes. Stops and thinks a while. Looks up dates on a calendar. Writes again.

Ellie and I switch to Uno and I win three games because she's watching Mom real close. She must be dying to see what's on those forms, too.

Finally, Mom stands up and heads for the door. "Be right back."

I'm standing at the desk one sec after the bathroom door shuts. "Keep watch," I order and grab the first form. Read fast and do not like what I'm reading. "Damn, this is bad."

"What?" Ellie says.

"She's writing down everything Dad's done to us since freakin' *Easter!* And she checked the boxes that say he can't come near us—any of us!"

Ellie rolls her eyes like I'm hopeless. "What did you expect? Was she supposed to *lie?*"

"But she's giving them dates, injuries, Brenda's phone number, the vet's number! They could be witnesses in court! There's nothing here about the good times we have with him—the vacations, the nights out, the way he comes to most of your games and my competitions!"

Ellie looks into the hall, then says, "So what? The good times don't make up for what he's turned into!"

"But on these forms he only sounds *bad.* If we can't see him 'til we're adults, it'll be *Mom's fault!*"

"Her fault we can't see him? *Her* fault he sounds bad? What planet are you living on? He *is* bad, especially to Mom! And he keeps getting worse!"

My stomach turns over. She's right. According to him, nothing is ever his fault. He says if we would just follow his rules and his life wasn't so stressful, he wouldn't have to "straighten us out." What he does to us is *our* fault, that's what he says. That's what he wants us to believe.

But I don't. That is so twisted, it's sick. I am not ending up like him. I won't if I think he's nuts, will I?

Ellie peeks into the hall again. Runs back to the card game. Motions for me to do the same, her hands flapping like wings. "Hurry up! She's coming back!" she whispers.

I quick make the court forms neat. Run over, drop to the floor and grab my cards. Just make it before Mom walks in. We finish our game like we don't know a thing about the court stuff.

Mom sits down at the desk and keeps working. Doesn't notice the forms are a little messed up.

Ellie has to keep nudging me. I can't pay attention to the game. I keep remembering the awful stuff Mom wrote about Dad, wonder how much more she's going to write.

What's killing me is that everything she wrote is true. It makes me face how awful Dad's been this year. Until I saw what she wrote, I forgot how many times she missed work, how tired we were in the morning because of their fights, how nice Dad acts in public and how mean he is in private.

I go back and forth. I hate him and fear him.

I miss him. Don't want to live with him. But is he all right?

What's wrong with me?

I drop my cards. "Let's quit for now, okay?"

Ellie stares at me. "Don't let it get to you. He can't hurt us now."

"No, but he can't help us, either."

She shrugs. "That's why we're here."

I feel too wiped out to climb up to the top bunk. Instead, I shove my stuff aside and crash on the bottom one. Pull my jacket over me and try to sleep.

No way. I lie there, remembering things I don't want to remember. Begin to wish I'd get zapped with killer lightning so I wouldn't have to deal with all this.

Finally, Mom says, "I'm done!" Checks her watch. "Oh my gosh, it's almost six! We'd better eat. Groups start at seven!"

Downstairs, a big pot of Indian rice and vegetables sits on the breakfast bar. Little Sheelpa's mother, Reena must have made supper. She's a vegetarian.

It smells good so I fill a plate. Tastes good, too, but I wish she'd thrown some meat in there. Bev must feel the same way because she asks, "Anybody want some hamburger to add to the rice?"

"Yeah!" three kids say and she heads for the kitchen.

Reena carries a plate to our table. Pulls a highchair over so she can feed Sheelpa.

"No offense," I tell her. "I like your food, but I'm a growing boy. Need my protein."

She smiles. "Then you're lucky I'm the cook tonight. My husband would make you eat whatever is on your plate."

"My dad's like that, too," Ellie says. "He's always gotta be the boss."

Reena nods. "But even the boss should respect what his family wants."

"Except he doesn't have to," I say.

Reena's eyebrows fly up. "Why not? Do you think only his wishes matter?"

I shrug.

"Sure he does," Ellie says. "Miguel's other name is Dad Junior."

"And your other name is Mom Junior!"

Mom stops eating. Knocks on the table twice. "Miguel, watch your temper."

Reena looks at me like I have two heads. "The man of the family can't be forced to respect his wife and kids. But I said he *should* respect them."

"I know," I say. "I'm sorry."

But that apology was too lame to fix what I did. Dad Talk. Talking like Dad.

I don't even agree with myself, with what I said. I know it's wrong Dad doesn't care what we want, but I sure can't change his mind.

8

Diego: *Hey. miss u so much. hows it goin?*

Ellie: *miguels still wacko. now he s playing detective.*

Diego: *huh?*

Ellie: *trying 2 find out what mom and the court advocate r planning.*

Diego: *4 real yur moms goin 2 court?*

Ellie: *yeah. she needs a protective order.*

Diego: *why? your dad dont know where she is.*

Ellie: *he knows where she works.*

Diego: *so what?*

Ellie: *so he could stalk her. attack her.*

Diego: *he wouldnt do that. he s a nice guy.*

Ellie: *how would u know? u think we made this up? left him for the fun of it?*

Diego: *i dont know.*

Ellie: *so what does that make me? a liar. stupid. what?*

Diego: *maybe u bugged him too much. made him lose it.*

Ellie: *see ya.*

Diego: *whats wrong?*

Ellie: *if yor on his side yor not on mine.*

Diego: *what did i say?*

Ellie:

Diego: *come on. i luv u. why do u think i m on his side?*

Ellie: *yor sucky attitude.*

Diego: *how about yor attitude? soon as we r apart u think i m bad. i m the enemy right?*

Ellie: *yor full of shit.*

Diego: *if u were here u wouldnt dis me like that.*

Ellie: *right. and u wouldnt dis me either becuz i would walk. see ya.*

Diego:

Ellie:

Diego: *luv u.*

Ellie:

DIEGO: *HEY, MR castillo. its diego.*

Dad: *how did you get my number?*

Diego: *ellie called u on my fone once.*

Dad: *oh. so how are u doing?*

Diego: *not so good. i dont know where ellie is and she wont give me her address.*

Dad: *i dont have it either. we had a couple accidents here sunday and ellie got hurt. now i m godzilla.*

Diego: *women sure over react. all i know is theyre in hawkinstown in some shelter.*

Dad: *thats more than i knew. thanks buddy. let me know if you find out anything else.*

Diego: *sure and u do the same 4 me ok?*

Dad: *deal.*

9

I'M NOT TOO popular around here. Reena and all The Girls think I'm a jerk, anti-women. And I guess I was—tonight.

I get tired of the shelter women badmouthing men nonstop. All men aren't bad. Even the bad ones aren't bad all the time. Of course, I don't know what goes on in everyone's house, either. Maybe a lot more men are nice in public like Dad and then treat their families like shit.

Anyway, The Girls are wrong about me, though it's my fault for shooting my mouth off. The truth is, I don't think men should force women to do what they want. Or say mean things. Or hurt them like Dad does just because they're bigger and stronger.

But I don't want to listen to them bashing men anymore so I'm heading for the living room, supper plate in hand.

Oops. Left too soon. The minute I sit on the couch, Bev sets a small bowl of cooked hamburger on every table.

I'm not proud. I go back to my table, spoon some meat on my rice, say, "Thanks, Bev."

"Uh, huh," she says, but doesn't look at me. I must be on her shit list, too.

When Ellie says, "Yeah, thanks a lot," Bev says, "My pleasure, girl. Remember, if you don't like what's for supper, there's always hamburger or hot dogs in the freezer. Chicken nuggets, too."

Ellie smiles. "You're the best!"

What's going on? At home, Ellie's the one who pouts and complains. Talks back to Dad. Breaks the rules. Me, I always try to say and do the right thing, especially with Dad.

Now it's switch time. Ellie's the brown nose and I'm the one in trouble! What's with that? Dad's not here to yell at her. She doesn't even have to be nice.

I notice it's almost 6:45 and the "outside" women and kids are already showing up for their groups. I finish my food, stick my plate and fork in the washer and head for the living room.

That's where the kids have to wait for the babysitters. Not that I want to go to groups, but it's a rule. Any kid under eighteen living in the shelter has to.

Next, the shelter moms drop their kids in the living room before they head downstairs for groups in Spanish or English. The little shelter kids are already in their pj's. That's gotta help upstairs at bedtime.

Bev comes over. Ignores me but sits her little twins on the couch. "Listen up. You are to behave yourselves, understand? I'd better not be pulled out of my group because you aren't listening to the babysitters!"

Georgie nods. "We'll be good." Roy's watching the new kids, finger in his mouth.

I take a chance. "How does it work," I ask Bev, "with the outside kids and moms? Do they have to keep things quiet, too?"

I hold my breath. Maybe she still won't talk to me.

She answers, "Same rules. Women can drive themselves here, but if they get a ride, they have to walk the last block. They're not allowed to give out our address or phone, either."

"That's good. Thanks." I slide further down the couch as more kids wander into the room. Georgie climbs on my lap, smiles at a new little girl. She's maybe two years old. Has perfect cornrows and brand-new jeans.

I count nine kids from the shelter, eleven from outside. All ages except babies under one. They go downstairs with their moms.

The new little girl and a boy about the same age start to cry when their moms leave. Georgie wiggles off my lap, does his hyper dance. The two watch him and quiet down. Nice work, Georgie! His twin brother Roy pokes the little boy, but stops when I tell him to.

A thin, serious-looking girl about twelve walks in. She sits on a chair near the couch and stares at the floor. Folds her hands like she's praying.

Carter strolls in, drops to his knees in front of her and makes a big show of bowing his head, making praying hands like hers. Then he looks at the girl and smirks.

She looks away, blinks her eyes like she's about to cry.

"Cut it out," I say.

He frowns and stands up. "You are such a wuss."

"I'd rather be a wuss than mean and a bully."

Before I can finish that discussion, two women show up. A couple kids run over and hug the older one. She hugs them back, looks around. "Hi, kids. I'm Asia and this is Cindy. We'll take care of you until the moms' meetings are over."

Asia picks up the new little girl who starts crying again. "How about we go to the playroom and have some fun, okay?"

The little girl pulls away, yells, "Where's Mama? I want Mama!"

"Don't worry," Asia purrs. "Mama will be back soon."

We follow Asia and Cindy down the hall to a big room. Another babysitter, a high school girl, is wiping off the tables. There's two couches on one wall. Round tables with plastic chairs in the middle of the room. Book shelves, dollhouse, cabinet, stuffed chair.

Asia claps her hands. "Okay, sit down at the tables, please." She pats her wiry salt-and-pepper hair. Waits until it's quiet. Takes attendance while Cindy reads the playroom rules.

Cindy's much younger than Asia and *hot*. Billy would drool, if I could tell him. Only he and the guys don't know where I am, and I don't plan to tell them any time soon.

Pilar calls some girls into her office. It's set in one corner, has a picture window, and must be soundproofed. I can't hear a word they're saying.

Asia claps her hands. "Okay, kids, listen up. I want you to choose something fun to do until you go to group." She looks at the teen sitter. "Josie will help you."

Kids who know the routine go straight to the dollhouse or toy cabinet so I check out the cabinet. On the lower shelves are Candyland, Chutes and Ladders, Old Maid.

No thanks. Higher up, I see playing cards, checkers, Uno and dominos. More like it. I look around for someone to play with but all the boys look a lot younger than me.

Kobi, Keesh's fourth grader, grabs a box of toy soldiers. "Hey Mike, wanna play war?"

What do you know, he actually called me Mike!

I shrug. "Sure."

He empties the box on the table. Shoves the green soldiers my way. "Here, you take these." He grabs the tan soldiers. Plus every last helicopter, airplane, jeep, and tank.

I stand up. "So I get some soldiers and you get everything else. What's with that?"

Kobi freezes. "Sorry, Mike. Here, how about you get half the jeeps and everything?" He looks scared, hyper alert. Looks like me when Dad's yelling or criticizing.

I remember being as small as Kobi and afraid of Dad. I wanted him to like me and like what I did, but I couldn't please him, no matter how hard I tried.

When I was six, I made him a Father's Day card from computer paper and crayons. Folded it in half. Covered the inside with a picture of Dad and me playing catch outside. Asked Mom how to spell "Happy Father's Day" right.

He smiled when I gave him the card, turned it over. Asked, "What, no envelope?"

I must have looked worried because he said, "Just kidding, okay?"

But the damage was done. I had forgotten to get an envelope. Mom and Ellie's cards were in envelopes. I was the only one who messed up on Dad's special day. I'd ruined it.

Kobi starts to toss his soldiers back in the box. Game over, he figures.

But I don't want his fear. I don't want him to think he'll never please me. "It's okay. Let's play. Your idea for divvying everything up even is good. Sorry, I over-reacted."

Kobi smiles. Probably not used to apologies. "It's okay," he mumbles.

We cover the table with soldiers, tanks, planes and whatnot in two opposing camps. I'm into it, all set to begin the countdown when Kobi jumps up.

"You're dead!" He yells and sweeps a tank through my troops.

My soldiers, tanks and planes fly everywhere. Most of them end up on the floor or in my lap. He's wrecked everything!

I straighten my arm and pull it through Kobi's battlefield. Now his soldiers and machines whip off the table. One soldier hits Kobi's neck.

"Ow!" He says. Blinks hard so he won't cry and rubs the spot.

"Sorry! I didn't mean to do that."

I hear Dad's voice. "Sorry, Mercedes. I was so stressed. I didn't mean it."

Asia hurries over. "No violence, remember? You two pick up the soldiers and put them back in the cabinet, *now*. Find something else to do."

"Sorry," I say. "I didn't hurt him on purpose."

"That's no excuse!"

Kobi's hands slap into begging position. "Asia, please give us another chance. We won't fight again, I promise!"

Fight? It wasn't a fight! He's covering for me!

"No, you won't," Asia says. "Because you two are done with the soldiers for tonight."

"You're mean!" Kobi yells and whacks the wall with his hand.

Asia frowns. "Maybe we should go upstairs and talk to your mom."

Kobi gets this *uh, oh* look on his face.

"No, no. I'm sorry! Sorry!" He picks up soldiers and artillery like his ass is on fire. I do the same, but slower. I want to show him it's all right, that she won't hurt us if we aren't speed demons.

I put the box of soldiers back in the cabinet and grab a box of dominoes.

Kobi stands there, looks sad. Waits to see if I'm done with him.

After my first promotion, Master Han said, *"Older students must help younger students. They must respect younger students. Compassion and understanding are a sign of the true martial artist."*

I'm glad he doesn't know what I just did.

I sit down at an empty table. Set up a long, curving line of dominos a quarter inch from each other. Kobi moves closer, asks, "Can I help?"

"Sure. Knock 'em over."

He smiles big. "Thanks!" Flicks the end domino so the line falls in a clattering, beautiful spiral.

Pilar steps out of her office, calls out the next group: Kobi, Kojo, Carter, and me.

In her office, we sit at a table in the middle of the room. Pilar gives us some forms and a pencil. While she explains how to fill them out, I watch Ellie through the window. She checks her caller ID three times. Steps into the hall to take the calls.

Cindy watches her. Says something to her after the third call.

Ellie rolls her eyes, shrugs. Sets a chair in the corner and sits on it. Next call, she turns the chair to the wall and her fingers fly.

A couple minutes later, I can tell something's wrong. She shakes her head, stands up. Flips the phone shut and shoves it in her pocket.

I wonder who's calling. Maybe her boss at camp. She missed work three days this week. Maybe he fired her.

She pulls her phone out again. Sits down and reads. Texts. Reads again. Looks at the ceiling. Closes her eyes and takes a deep breath.

I jump when Pilar says, "Mike, you're not writing. Are you okay?"

"Sure. Sorry, Pilar."

Carter makes a "Duh!" face—eyes crossed, tongue hanging out. Nice guy. I could put him in his place with a couple good pinches under the table. Hear Master Han say, *"Above all, avoid unnecessary violence."*

I shrug, look right at Carter. "Nobody's perfect."

Pilar nods. "You are so right, Mike."

I pick up my pencil. The top of the form reads, SAFETY PLAN. We're supposed to put down different ways to stay safe at home. Or how to get away if we're not safe.

Sorry Pilar, but I don't think there's a safety plan on earth that will work when Dad's in Dictator Mode. When he walks in the door like that, we're not safe. Period.

I fill out the form anyway. If there was time, I'd run to my room and hide under my bed. Or run out the kitchen door if Dad wasn't in front of it. If I made it upstairs, I could lock myself in the bathroom and call 911. If he didn't knock the door down or take my phone.

It's hard to plan ahead with someone like Dad, but I did realize there were different ways to escape from him. I don't think I'd sit there and watch a disaster unfold, if something like Sunday afternoon ever happened again.

If we're ever home again on Sunday, that is. With Dad.

After group, Ellie and I use the bathroom in the hall. Who knows when it will be available again?

The dining and living rooms are already buzzing with women and kids. The babysitters gave us a snack, but I'm hungry again.

I grab some cookies from a package on the counter, give a couple to Ellie. She takes one bite, then crumbles them like she's in a zone. Her eyes never leave the uncovered windows across from her. They're black now that it's dark. Behind Ellie's reflection are streetlights and speeding headlights. I don't think she sees them.

"Did your boss call tonight?" I ask. Try to sound casual because I want to know who called so many times. Don't think it was her boss.

"No, my boss is being nice about this."

Mom sits down. Says nothing. She clasps her hands together, stares at them like she's about to pray. Or cry.

A baby shrieks and two kids fight over a toy. Holly tells Bev, "Group was kind of fun."

Mom hears nothing. She's left the planet. Ellie touches her arm. "How was your group?" Mom startles, frowns at Ellie like she's been asleep. Doesn't answer.

"Is it okay if we go upstairs with Keesh or Bev?" Ellie asks.

Mom stands slowly, like someone's holding her down. "No, I'll take you."

In the room, she kicks off her shoes and crawls into bed. Falls asleep immediately.

We slip off our shoes and slide under the covers, too.

Wouldn't Dad have a fit if he saw us go to bed completely dressed.

But he's not here and Mom's out of it.

It feels like no one's in charge.

10

DIEGO: *HEY. R u my sweet girl again?*

Ellie: *not if u still think i m a liar.*

Diego: *i never sed that. whats wrong with u?*

Ellie: *i m mad u dont believe dad s an asshole.*

Diego: *hey all i no is what u told me. he helps u with math. pays the bills. gives your mom a car and a nice house.*

Ellie: *and that means he can do whatever he wants.*

Diego: *where wood you guys be if he didnt take care of u?*

Ellie: *mom works full time but he takes her paycheck. gives her an allowance. how can she buy anything 4 us?*

Diego: *but he makes more money rite? so he handles the finances. whats wrong with that?*

Ellie:

Diego: *thats how it should be.*

Ellie:

ELLIE: *HEY GIRLFRIEND. what up?*

Florie: *cant beleeve rachel and jorge r pregnant.*

Ellie: *since when? i been out of touch.*

Florie: *u got that rite. rachel s eight weeks gone. why didnt diego tell u? he s tite with jorge.*

Ellie: *mayb cuz i m not talking to him right now. he s been an asshole lately.*

Florie: *wow. i saw him yesterday an he was so nice. why u mad at him?*

Ellie: *i told u why. hey u think he s so great u can have him.*

Florie: *thank u and goodbye. i m about to burn up his fone line.*

Ellie: *slow down. we r not breaking up. i just hate his macho attitude.*

Florie: *get used to it. why do you think rachel is pregnant?*

Ellie: *could it be sex.*

Florie: *o ha ha. yeah. the jorge way. sex or i dump u girl.*

Ellie: *diego tried that. i said no no and no.*

Florie: *girl you crazy. if he asked me to do it i would be like tell me when.*

Ellie: *find your own boy toy.*

Florie: *i have one but hector is no toy. gotta go. working overtime.*

Ellie: *see ya soon i hope.*

Florie: *you better.*

DIEGO: *HEY.*

Ellie: *why u calling me? i m just a useless female.*

Diego: *no yor not. i m sorry baby. i can be so stupid when i m upset.*

Ellie: *thats no excuse. i am plenty upset these days but i dont insult u.*

Diego: *i sed i was sorry.*

Ellie: *fine. just dont dis me or my mom again.*

Diego:

Ellie: *and another thing. dont call me so much. you pissed off the babysitters last nite.*

Diego: *what do you care? you dont need no babysitter.*

Ellie: *they r nice but they dont like a lot of outside calls. why should i hassle em?*

Diego: *fine. i wont call so much. but it s hard. i think about u all the time.*

Ellie: *same here.*

Diego: *then why cant we talk wen we want? or mayb u dont want 2. r u breaking up with me? u better say no or i will kill myself.*

Ellie: *dont say that. u know i luv u. i just cant take a lot of calls. let me call u first ok?*

Diego: *oh i get it. u can call me wenever u want. but i cant call u. that is cold.*

Ellie: *try 2 understand. fone calls make the women here nervous.*

Diego: *what about me? with u gone i m a wreck. i want 2 drive in 2 a tree.*

Ellie:

Diego: *u there.*

Ellie: *yeah. but stop talking like that.*

Diego: *then stop yelling at me for loving u so much.*

Ellie: *prove it. dont call me every twenty minutes.*

Diego: *all rite but i want your cell bill next time we go out.*

Ellie: *ok. if I have it. it goes to a post office box first. and remember if u pay my bill u cant tell miguel or mom.*

Diego: *u got it.*

Ellie: *btw i m going back 2 camp 2 morrow. just one prob. i have no clean clothes.*

Diego: *so wash them tonite. we r goin out 2 morrow. rite.*

Ellie: *sure if i can get a washer and dryer. call u later. luv u lots.*

Diego: *luv u and miss you. want r old life back so bad.*

Ellie: *me 2.*

11

I FELT ANTSY when I woke up this morning. Wanted so bad to forget what happened yesterday, but I couldn't.

That's when Mom went to court and got a temporary restraining order and temporary custody of us kids. The court said Dad can't come near Mom or us.

I know this will sound weird after what Dad did, but sometimes I kind of want to see him. I don't want to move back home or anything, just want to know if he's okay. He could get hit by a truck and we wouldn't even know!

Mom doesn't agree. When she got back from court, we sat down in the living room with her. "Kids, I'm sorry," she said, "but there won't be any visits with your dad for now."

She dropped this bomb with her friend Keesh sitting next to her. Said it exactly like Dad used to say, 'No discussion.'

"Why can't Ellie and I visit him?" I asked. "You don't have to go with us."

Ellie rolled her eyes. "Are you nuts? You know he will interrogate us if we visit. He'll twist what we say and pressure us to testify against Mom."

"How would you know?"

"How come you *don't* know?"

Keesh moved closer to Mom on the couch.

"Miguel, that's enough!" Mom said. "There will be no visits with Dad. It's done. You need to change your attitude or you can stay home from camp tomorrow."

I took a deep breath, talked softer. "I'm sorry, Mom, but it seems like you and Ellie exaggerate everything. You make Dad sound like Monster of The World. Do you really think he'll torture and threaten us if we eat lunch with him once a week?"

"Yes!" She and Ellie said together.

Keesh nodded. I knew she was sitting with Mom to help her stay tough about Dad, but I resented it. Keesh needs to take care of her own situation and keep her nose out of ours.

No, I take that back. What Keesh does won't really matter because The Girls outnumber me anyway. Mom's acting pretty tough right now, but I wonder how she'll be the next time she goes to court and actually has to face Dad. Next time she'll go for permanent custody, and I guarantee Dad will hire the best lawyer he can get. I also guarantee he'll fight to keep custody of us, too.

Okay, I can't guarantee that, but I think he will.

So I lie in bed, thinking about all that could happen when they meet in court. I roll over, close my eyes against the sun. Try to relax.

Can't go back to sleep.

I'm almost glad when Ellie whispers, "Hey, want to run?"

"Is that allowed?"

"Bev walks three mornings a week."

"Okay, but you gotta promise—no talking about Dad."

"No prob."

We pull on shorts and tees under the covers. Tip-toe past Mom's bed, carrying our sneakers. She's been so stressed lately. Don't want to wake her up.

On the stairs I check my watch. "Guess we can only run for a half hour."

"Yeah, especially since we've gotta find the camp bus stop."

"And eat breakfast."

Eye roll and head shake. "Are you ever not hungry?"

I ignore that and charge into the office. There's a new woman at the front desk. She's lily white with straight hair the color of sand. When she sees us, she smiles. "Hi, kids. I'm Dawn. What can I do for you?"

"We want to run before breakfast. Is that okay?"

Dawn looks unsure. "I don't know. Is it okay with your mother?"

"She won't care," I say. "We run three, four times a week at home."

"And she's sound asleep," Ellie adds. "Went to court yesterday. We don't want to bother her."

Dawn shrugs. "Okay. I guess it's alright if you watch your backs. Make sure you're not followed and keep an eye out for familiar cars or people. I can lend you a phone with 911 on it if you don't have one."

I hold mine up. "No need, thanks."

Dawn's phone rings. "See you later. Remember to sign out."

I scribble our names on the sheet in the hall. Hope Mom can read them.

The city streets are already baking. It can't be this hot at home, but who knows? The shelter TV is almost never tuned to news or weather. We hardly ever see a newspaper, either. It's like living in a cave.

"We'd better find the new bus stop for camp first," Ellie says. "It's supposed to be near the Drop-In Mart."

We run a couple minutes and Ellie says, "Hold it." She stands on tiptoe. Reads a small sign nailed to a telephone pole. "Yup, this is it. Now we can run the other way."

Three minutes later, we see the Golden Arches. "Hey, smell the peppers and sausage," I say. "Got some cash?"

"Yeah, but not for McDonald's. I need school clothes."

"Mom will help you."

"I don't think so. She has to pay for insurance and gas and save for an apartment. I've gotta get a job."

"Me, too. Look at these sneakers. They're getting tight and the soles are wearing out. But how can I earn money? I'm fifteen. Nobody will hire me."

My brain spits out a picture of women going through donation bags in the living room. I do not plan to get "new" shoes that way. The stuff people give us is clean and in good shape, but I've never seen anyone but women go through the bags.

I don't plan to start a trend, either especially with Rock Star Carter watching. Guess I'll wear my holey sneakers until they fall off or Mom has cash, whichever comes first.

Ellie shrugs. "Maybe she'll have some money saved by the time we start school."

We take off again, side-by-side. At home, we run in the street, but here that would be suicidal. City streets are jammed with traffic.

So are the sidewalks. We switch to single file when a boy on a bike plows by. Stay that way to avoid a wide stroller, a girl rollerblading, and a very drunk old man.

My throat's dry and my tee already soaked with sweat.

Two stinky buses rumble past. Make me cough so hard I bend over and hack.

"Let's go back and have breakfast," Ellie says. "This isn't much fun."

She slows to a walk, looks around. "Have you been watching for Dad's truck?"

"No, but it shouldn't be hard to spot."

His truck is a six-year-old blue Silverado in mint condition. Eight-foot bed, big decal on the back window. Fishing poles and tackle box on the cab floor.

He's so freakin' proud of that box. Painted the top himself: a white water stream in the woods and a big rainbow trout fighting at the end of a line. Looks professional and perfect, like almost everything he does.

Ellie puffs out a big sigh. "I hate this. We can't even run without worrying that Dad will show up."

"He'd better not. If he breaks the restraining order, he could go to jail."

"I know, but do you want to be the one to turn him in?"

"Don't think so."

A big blue truck slows down across the street.

My heart speeds up and Ellie's face fades to pale. "Oh my God. Is that him?" she croaks.

I sneak another look, trip on a crack in the sidewalk. "No. It's not a Silverado. Probably some guy with the hots for you."

"Whew, that's okay then. But don't tell Diego, okay? He's the jealous type."

"Why would he care if some stranger checks you out?"

She blushes. "Because he gets jealous if anyone looks at me. It's kind of sweet."

"Sweet? You're afraid to tell him something and that's *sweet?*"

She wipes her wet face on her sleeve. "Forget it. You're too young to understand."

Looks at her watch. "Whooee, we are running late! Gotta shower before camp."

"Thanks for changing the subject, *Mom.*"

And then it hits me. "We've missed almost a week of camp and we're taking a different bus today. How do we explain that?"

She starts running again. "I told my boss you got an ear infection from Billy's pool and I had to stay home with you. Make sure you tell the same story, okay?"

"Sure, but how do I explain the new bus to kids who ask?"

"Remind them camp employees sometimes get assigned to a different bus."

"I'm not a camp employee."

"No, but Mom makes us to ride together in case she has to pick us up."

"Yeah, that works."

She grabs my arm. "Look out!"

Oops—stray dog pooping on the sidewalk.

"Thanks. By the way, when did you become such an awesome liar?"

She smiles. "I've *always* been an awesome liar!"

I don't smile back. "I guess so. You sure kept me out of the loop when you and Mom were thinking of leaving Dad."

She ignores my comment. "Which reminds me. We're supposed to be watching for him. You take this side. I'll go across the street."

We slow down. Scan parked and moving cars. Check out people on the sidewalk and the street.

This spy stuff would be exciting if I wasn't so damn scared.

I mean, what would I do if Dad actually showed up? Take off? Call 911? Jump in the truck and leave with him?

Oh, yeah, now there's a good idea. Dad and I will both be breaking the restraining order!

Ellie checks her watch as I punch in my code at the shelter door. "We messed up—didn't leave enough time for a shower and breakfast."

We run upstairs. There's only one bathroom free!

"Now what?" I ask.

Ellie thinks, raises her finger. "Okay, listen. I'll jump in the shower. You grab clean clothes and towels for both of us and leave mine outside the bathroom door. I'll shower and dress fast and then it's your turn."

Sixteen minutes later we're both clean, downstairs, and looking for food. Mom is eating corn flakes. With a really ripe banana.

At least she looks better than last night. Actually smiles when I tell her about our run and quick showers. "I can't believe it!" she says. "Both of you made it in and out of the shower in less than hour? I'm holding you to that when we have our own place. Especially on school days."

Ellie giggles. "Sure you will, Mom."

Our own place. Probably a two- or three-bedroom apartment. Hope it's three so we can have our own rooms again.

I cook fast, too, and set a record: four perfect fried egg sandwiches in ten minutes. Three for me and one for Ellie.

"Awesome breakfast, Miguel," Ellie says, licking ketchup off her finger. "I could eat this every day."

"I'll make it every day if you call me Mike."

Ellie rolls her eyes.

Jenna sits down with a bagel. "Sounds like a good breakfast plan, as long as we don't run out of eggs. Sometimes we have to scrounge for food stamps at the end of the month."

Ellie lifts an eyebrow. "Then I guess we won't make a habit of eating three egg sandwiches at one time, right Miguel?"

My turn to ignore her, since she won't call me Mike.

"What's the rush? You guys goin' to day camp?" Jenna asks.

Ellie nods. "Yeah, I'm an assistant counselor."

I look at the clock, jump up. "Ellie, we're about to miss the bus!"

Ellie looks at Mom. "Will you...?"

"Go ahead, I'll do the dishes."

I eat my last sandwich running to the Mart.

The bus interrogation isn't too bad. Luckily, we only know a couple kids. Ellie and I stick to our story, and they buy it.

I admit Ellie's better at lying than me, but all this practice helps. By the time we go home, I should be at her level—professional, assuming I dare lie to Dad.

It's easy to figure out who calls Ellie before the bus even rolls into camp. She sounds all lovey-dovey, laughing and shit, and she's only that way with Diego.

Pretty soon, though, she's frowning. "I don't know about tonight. I still have to do my laundry. Everything's dirty. I have nothing to wear."

She turns her back to me and whispers. I hear every word. "I'm not trying to hassle you, Dee! How about tomorrow night? Oh. No, I can't do lunch today. I have to watch the kids."

She winces, holds the phone away from her ear. Diego is yelling at her!

Nobody besides me notices, of course. The bus is louder than a rock concert.

When the yelling stops, she says, "Later," and hangs up.

About time. If this is love, how come it's so nasty?

Her phone rings again. She checks the caller. Turns it off, drops it in her purse. Looks out the window. A tear rolls down her cheek.

"What's with all the yelling?" I ask.

She shrugs, wipes off the tear. "Diego's got one night off this week and this is it. We were supposed to go out."

"So do your laundry after camp."

"I'll try, but you know how hard it is to get the machines. Look what I had to wear today."

She's right. Last year's flowery shorts and a too-tight top. Not good.

"I've gotta wash my clothes tonight no matter what, even after lights out if I have to!"

"Be careful. You could get a warning for that."

Her shoulders slump. "I know."

Maybe I can snag her a machine before supper.

Her phone clatters against something in her purse. She grabs it, checks the message. Starts texting. Reads, frowns, types. Reads again. Smiles and signs off. "Dee apologized and said he'll take me to the Laundromat before supper." Big sigh. "He is so sweet."

He's not sweet. He's slick. She can't go out unless she does her laundry, right? So he's taking her to a Laundromat. Well, *duh!*

Her phone vibrates again as we pull into Big Sky.

I love the place. Nothing's changed since we started coming here six years ago. Nothing needs to change, either. Big pool, picnic tables, playground, lodge for rainy days.

Ellie answers her phone. Listens, smiles, looks at me. "I'll ask him. Miguel, you want to go to Brenda's house with Diego and me on Saturday? We can visit Moochie and Dee says he'll give you a Tae Kwon Do lesson."

"Sure!" Didn't know Dee's into martial arts, too.

Ellie smiles. "Thanks, Dee. Miguel's in. See you Saturday at the Mart."

Wait a sec.

"How does Diego know where Moochie is?" I ask after she hangs up. "And is it safe for me to hang out at my *dojang?*"

"No, we can't go anywhere near Master Han's because Dad might be watching the place. That's why Diego's giving you the lesson, not Master Han. And I told him Brenda has Moochie."

"Oh, that's keeping things confidential. Ya know, I'd like to talk to Master Han, but we're not supposed to tell anyone *anything,* remember?"

Her eyes get that "One more word and you're dead" look. "Diego is no snitch, okay?"

I shut up because I need to see my dog and I want a Tae Kwon Do lesson, even if it isn't with Master Han. Even if I'm getting the lesson from someone who doesn't seem a whole lot like him.

The bus stops inside the camp gate and kids file off real fast.

Ellie's phone rings. I stand up. "Ignore it. We gotta go."

She answers it, frowns. "Oh, sorry. I forgot to tell you. The Mart is on the corner of Wooster and Main. See you later. Just look for the girl with the Snoopy laundry bag."

Now there's only one kid left on the bus besides us—a cranky white boy who never smiles and moves slower than mud. As he passes our seat, he slows down even more and stares. We stare back and he finally slithers out the bus.

The bus driver writes something on his pad. I tap Ellie's shoulder. "Come on, we gotta get off the bus or we'll get a write-up!"

She lifts her finger, mouths, "Wait!"

Turns back to the phone. "Don't give me a hard time, Dee. The only place you can pick us up is the Drop-In Mart!"

Her fingers tap the seat in front of ours. She rolls her eyes, starts to talk. Shuts up. Tries again. Sighs.

The bus driver turns around. I hold up my hand. "Just one more minute, okay?"

"No, I have to return the bus, *now.*"

I think about getting off alone but I don't. I gotta see this. Ellie's getting good and mad and she won't back off like Mom usually does with Dad.

"Fine," she shouts. "You back to that subject again? Forget about tonight."

What did I tell you?

She stares at her phone, mouth open. "The jerk! He hung up on me!"

12

ELLIE: *WHAT?*

Diego: *u still in a nasty mood?*

Ellie: *yor the one who keeps bugging me for my address. the one who hung up.*

Diego: *ok ok. sorry. i will pick u up at the drop in mart tonite at 5. u happy now?*

Ellie: *no. your attitude sucks. u live with your mom an do what u want. i follow shelter rules or i m homeless.*

Diego: *no prob. if u get kicked out of the shelter u can move in with me.*

Ellie: *forget it. i told u no sex and no babies. i m goin to college. i mean it.*

Diego: *fine. then we visit the clinic. get the pill. evrybody does it.*

Ellie: *you mean like jorge and rachel?*

Diego: *hey they messed up. it happens.*

Ellie: *well i m not messing up. so if u want sex go find a slut with yor values.*

Diego: *ok. forget the pill.*

Ellie: *u mean it?*

Diego: *yeah.*

Ellie: *no more pressure. u gotta promise.*

Diego: *i promise. cant wait 2 see u 2 nite. i miss u so much it hurts.*

Ellie: *me 2.*

      ✌   ✌   ✌

DAD: *HOW'S IT going diego. you find out where my family is yet? i miss them a lot.*

Diego: *no but i keep trying.*

Dad: *thanks. esp. since mercedes fixed it so i cant see the kids.*

Diego: *for real.*

Dad: *yeah. i work all day. go home to an empty house and eat crap.*

Diego: *that is so wrong. dads should know where their kids r. i should know where my girl is. at least me and ellie are goin out tonite. i mite learn somethin.*

Dad: *let me know ok?*

Diego: *no prob. us men gotta stick together.*

Dad: *exactly. keep in touch.*

Diego: *u got it.*

MIGUEL: *HEY BILLY. i lost my fone an ellie wont let me use hers. had to sneak it when she was asleep. we mite go to the cape for a couple weeks. use my uncle's cottage. i will try to borrow moms fone. Ttyl*

13

IT SUCKS LIVING in a shelter during summer vacation. Camp helps, but not much. There's nothing to do around here except shoot hoops in the back yard. And it's not much fun to play with little guys who can't even get the ball in the basket.

Even school's starting to look good to me, and I hate school! Especially homework.

Here's how bored I am. At 5:45 p.m. I had nothing better to do than walk Ellie to the Mart.

"Thanks," she said when we were almost there. "I don't like walking alone in the city."

Her laundry bag bounces on her back. Looks heavy, but I don't make any offers. She's touchy about accepting help.

I scan the street. "You afraid Dad will show up?"

"Yeah, but mostly I hate the boys around here. They creep me out, they're so pushy. In fact, the ones who try the hardest look twenty years old!"

"They probably are. They like fresh meat."

"You're disgusting."

"No, realistic. These guys don't want any nasty diseases."

She sticks a finger in her mouth like she wants to vomit.

I punch the walk light. Wait a while. Finally we get the "go" signal. Turns out that gives us maybe twenty seconds to cross the street.

Which is not enough since two or three cars always run the red light.

Today, one of them is a black BMW. Screeches to a stop two feet from us.

"Asshole!" Ellie yells.

He gives her the bird and roars away.

My heart's beating like crazy. "Where are the cops when you need them?"

"Good luck with that." She shifts the laundry bag to the other shoulder. "I hate the city. It's too loud and too crowded. I wish we were home, minus Dad, of course."

"Me, too. At least I could go to Tae Kwon Do, and you'd have soccer this fall."

Ellie snorts. "Big whoop."

"What do you mean?"

"Is that all that's important, sports? If we move back, Mom will let Dad stay, I know she will. You want to live with him again?"

"I don't know."

"Still on a different planet, huh?"

We stop talking.

Finally, I say, "So you and Diego are doing your laundry and then going out to eat?"

Ellie smiles, walks faster. "Yeah, he's good to me."

"I'd agree if he was feeding me, too."

Shelter food is not the best, unless Mom, Bev, or Keesh is cooking. Somebody said we're having baked chicken tonight.

When I get back, I check out the kitchen and the food smells so good I bet Keesh made it.

Only I don't see her. In fact, there aren't any moms in the kitchen. A kid's crying in the living room, though. I peek in.

Carter is hiding behind a chair. He waits a few seconds, then jumps at a baby boy sitting on the couch. He gets in the kid's face, snarls and makes ugly faces. What a jerk! The kid is maybe a year old!

I walk in, grab his arm and pull him away. "Wow, Carter. You are such a brave guy—scaring a baby."

He lifts his chin, smiles. "Hey, what up Mr. Hero?"

"Drop the charm, pretty boy. That works with the girls but not me. How come you're taking care of a baby? Excuse me, *torturing* a baby?"

He shrugs. "Got nothing better to do."

The baby sucks his thumb and stops wailing. Watches both of us like we're about to toss a bomb his way.

I grab a truck and some blocks off the shelves and sit down next to him. Smile, give him the truck. He grabs a block and bangs them together. Smiles at me.

"Gee, that was hard, wasn't it, Carter? And I didn't even have to scare him."

Carter claps slowly. "Woo Hoo! Whadda guy!"

Jayda hurries in with a sippee cup and picks up the baby. "Hi, Donnie! Bet you've been having fun." She looks closer, wipes his cheeks. "No, looks like he was crying and you made him happy. Thanks, Carter."

"Anytime, Jayda," he says with his wide smile. "You know I love little kids."

Me, I'm not smiling. "Um, sorry to have to tell you this, Jayda, but Carter was scaring your baby when I walked in."

Carter gets in my face, or tries to. He's six inches shorter than me. "Why are you lying like that? You're the nasty one, always yelling at women around here."

"Yeah, sometimes. But I own up to it and apologize! You didn't do that. You're like my Dad! He's rotten when no one's looking!"

Jayda stares at me, then Carter. Doesn't seem to know what to think.

Mom walks in slowly. Looks exhausted. Comes into the living room and sits down. "It's mighty quiet in here. What's going on?"

Jayda shifts Donnie to her other hip. "Mike says Carter was scaring my Donnie."

Carter's mouth drops and he opens his palms like Mr. Innocence. "I wasn't, ma'am. I *swear*. I would never hurt a baby."

Mom frowns. "I guess it's one word against the other, then. You seem polite, Carter, but here's the thing, Jayda. My son has his faults, but lying is not one of them."

Jayda sighs. "I am so disappointed in you, Carter. I 'spose I'll have to take Donnie everywhere I go."

"Not if I'm here," Mom says. "I'll be happy to watch him."

"Thanks," Jayda says, but a tear rolls down her face. "I just want him to be safe, ya know?"

Mom waits until Jayda leaves, then says, "I'd better not hear the word 'scaring' along with your name, Carter, or I will tell everyone about today, including your mother!"

Carter tries one more time. "See what you did to me, Mike? What did I do to you?"

"Remember knocking over your brother's milk on purpose the other day? Well, this is strike two. Think about it."

"Liar." Carter says softly. "Excuse me, ma'am. I need to see if Mom needs any help upstairs."

After he leaves, Mom shakes her head. "He's a piece of work, but he's right about one thing. You do need to watch your temper, especially with the women."

"I know, but thanks for believing me anyway. Want me to fix us both a plate? Supper smells good tonight."

She smiles for the first time. "That would be great, thanks."

I fill our plates with baked chicken from the oven and rice and beans on the stove. "How was work?" I ask when we start eating.

Her tired eyes come back. She shakes her head, pushes her plate away. "Not good. Dad started harassing me at lunch."

I get visions of him stalking her in the cafeteria. "What happened?"

"He kept calling my desk and hanging up."

"How do you know it was him?"

"Who else would ring my extension, hear my voice and hang up four times in ten minutes?"

I shrug. "I don't know. Could be anyone. Salesman with a hangover, wrong number."

"Fine, call me paranoid, but I watch for Dad's truck every time I'm on the road, and you'd better do the same."

"Ellie and I did this morning when we ran. No sign of him."

Mom picks at her food. "So far, but you know he's looking for us. He doesn't give up easy."

Word.

After supper, Jenna and I play checkers. My mind is still on Dad going to Mom's office, so Jenna beats me like I never played the game before. I'm saved from total humiliation when Ellie staggers into the dining room. She's carrying a tall pile of folded laundry and the top half is tilting bad.

"Oops! Gotta help Ellie. Thanks for the game, Jenna."

I grab the top half of the pile and set it on a chair.

"Thanks." Ellie looks around. Spots Mom in the kitchen talking to Bev and Keesh. "Hey, Mom! We've gotta go upstairs, put the laundry away, okay?"

Mom raises a finger. "Hold on. Wait for Keesh."

Keesh retrieves Kobi and Kojo from the living room. Upstairs, Ellie closes our door. We set the laundry on Mom's bed. I'm surprised when Ellie doesn't immediately put it away. She'd never admit it, but she's almost as anal as Dad.

Instead, she sits on her bed, stares at the wall.

"So how was your date?"

She shrugs. Opens her purse, pulls out a 'doggie box' and plastic fork.

Yum. I smell garlic, cheese, Italian sauce.

She gives it to me. "I couldn't finish my chicken parm and pasta."

"Hey, thanks!" I take it, notice her eyes are puffy, eyelids red.

I don't ask. Diego is her business. I sit at the end of her bed and chow. "Mmmmm. This is great," I mumble, my mouth full. "Supper was good tonight, but this is so much better."

Oops. She starts crying buckets.

I stop eating. "What's wrong?"

She wipes her eyes, blows her nose. "Diego, that's what. According to him, I couldn't do one thing right. I used too much soap in the machines. I couldn't make the washer and dryer go faster. I folded the clothes sloppy. I changed in the laundromat bathroom and he wanted me to change again. Said my top was too sexy. I wouldn't do it and he got real mad. Wouldn't talk to me in the restaurant until I put my elbows on the table. Then he yelled at me! I was so embarrassed. Everyone was looking. "

He's nuts. The top wasn't that low cut, though it showed a little skin at the waist. "What's eating him, treating you like that?"

She shrugs. "I don't know. He had a bad week at home. I don't want to talk about it." She shucks her shoes. Slides under the covers and pulls them over her head.

"So our visit Saturday with Moochie is off?"

No answer.

I put her clothes away. Fold any that got unfolded. Make neat piles in her drawers. At least she won't have to go nuts in the morning looking for something to wear. Maybe she'll even smile.

Me, I'm out of clean socks and shorts. Guess it's my turn to fight for the machines.

Turns out I'm a natural slob without Mom doing all the laundry and Dad continually on my ass. No excuse for it, considering I have two beds to call my own and the bottom one always looks like a Salvation Army bin.

Which is not good. Nadia inspects the bedrooms two, three times a week. Unannounced. And she likes things neat. So Mom has issued her threat: "You kids get me a warning for a messy room and you're grounded for two days."

Don't want that again. I shovel out my bottom bunk. Wiggle around under the bed retrieving laundry and other stuff. Hide some of it in my backpack.

Then I climb onto my top bunk. It's too early to go to sleep but I don't feel like reading or playing with my Game Boy. Instead, I stare at the ceiling until I'm in a zone. Jump when Ellie starts talking.

I thought she was asleep.

"Here's another problem. Diego is still asking me for the shelter address. I won't tell him, and he won't let it go. I think that's why he was so nasty tonight. After the way he treated me at the laundromat I didn't want to rile things up again, so I took his mean talk at the restaurant, too. I did Mom's old thing—stopped talking. I guess I messed up."

She sits up, fully dressed, shoulders slumped.

I stare at her. "You were trying to keep the peace, I get that. But he should stop bugging you for the address! You can't do it. It's a *rule!* What's so hard for him to understand? Why does he keep pushing you for it? Maybe he just wants an excuse to crap on you."

Ellie shrugs, looks demolished.

This is not my sister. She stood up to Dad sometimes, and I never dared do that. She dumped boys who bugged her too much. And I heard her yell at Dee plenty of times when he was being a jerk.

Why doesn't she get that Diego's anger is not her fault?

She looks so sad, I don't even bother to nag.

"Listen, don't worry about Saturday," I say. "I'll ask Mom to drive us to Brenda's. She must be dying to see Moochie, too."

"Bad idea. She's so stressed out it's scary. Haven't you noticed how she's shaking a lot and forgetting stuff and losing things? She forgot to take her lunch to work yesterday and can't find her copies of the court papers. Besides, she can't give you a Tae Kwon Do lesson."

I sit up so fast I almost whack my head on the ceiling. "Oh, yeah. I forgot. Where's he planning to give me the lesson?"

"Our back yard 'cause it's bigger than Brenda's."

"Huh? Did you tell him about..."

"The restraining order? Yeah, I told him we can't go home in case Dad's there. He said, 'Who cares, no one will find out!' That did it. I told him to forget the whole thing: Brenda's, the Tae Kwon Do lesson, us."

"Gee, thanks." And then I remember what Master Han always says. *"Do, the way of life in Tae Kwon Do, involves responsibility for yourself and others."*

How fast I've forgotten what he taught us.

"I'm sorry, Ellie. You were right to cancel on him. He shouldn't ask you to do bad things. Or get mad when you won't."

She sighs. "Yeah. He's been so different lately. I hate when he acts like this."

"I thought he was your sweetheart."

Ellie flops back down on her pillow. "He was, when he was sweet and kind and fun. My girlfriends loved him, too. Then he got upset about his parents' break up and summer school and us moving out. He's changed, a lot and I don't know how to handle it."

"It's his problem, not yours! Maybe he misses Dad. He really likes him."

"I never thought of that, but yeah, that could be another thing."

"And that's not your fault. Neither is how he has to go to summer school or that you can't tell him where you are."

She wipes her eyes. "I know, but I'm not perfect, either. Sometimes I bug him."

"So? Right now he's the one treating you mean and pumping you for our address!"

She sighs. "You're right, but I miss him every day anyway, even when I'm mad at him. I don't know how to feel."

"Why don't you talk to Florie?"

Ellie rolls her eyes. "Waste of time. She thinks Dee is soooo fine."

"Then talk to Pilar."

"I dunno. Maybe."

Her phone rings. She checks the caller. Flips it closed.

"Diego?"

"Yeah."

One knock and in walks Mom. "It's almost quiet time, kids."

That means in five minutes, moms will say goodnight and take their kids to the room. Babies will stop crying and kids will stop yelling. Doors will close. Noise will fade to a hum.

I lie there and wait for it.

Mom turns off the light, opens our windows a crack.

Cool, fresh air blows on my face. Narrow branches and small leaves dance in the moonlight on our wall. It's not home, but it's the same moon and sky.

Ellie blows her nose and sniffles. Flops around like she can't get comfortable.

Mom goes right to sleep. I still want to talk to her about Ellie's problems, even if Ellie would kill me for it. But Mom has too many problems of her own. These days she's in a zone half the time—worrying, confused.

The rest of the time she switches to fast forward and picks The Girls' brains non-stop. That's when she's ultra-focused on getting us an apartment and all the court stuff.

I never know which way she'll be, though. I just know she's too busy talking to Marsha and the other women to notice what's happening to Ellie and me. We're on our own.

I follow the ceiling crack over my bed to a place in the corner where the ceiling squares don't quite meet the sheetrock. There's bruised paint under the windows and gouges in the floor.

What a list Dad would make if he inspected our room.

Our quiet, safe, imperfect room.

14

DIEGO: *ELLIE. ITS been 2 days. get over it.*

Ellie:

Diego: *ok. i admit i was a jerk at the londromat and restrant.*

Ellie:

Diego: *i will never yell at u like that again. i promise. 4 give me please.*

Ellie:

Diego: *come on. evryone makes mistakes.*

Ellie:

Diego: *i flunked 2 tests 2day. dont u even care?*

Ellie: *is that my fault 2?*

Diego: *no. i worked real late last nite. didnt study. why should i? my uncle has a job 4 me in construction. but mom will kick me out if i quit school.*

Ellie: *so dont. graduate. make more money later.*

Diego: *u sound like my mother.*

Ellie: *so what? the other nite you sounded like my father.*

Diego: *sorry. but u know i m not a patient person so why did u bug me? why did u do everything in slow motion?*

Ellie: *because i dont get enuf sleep. i m tired all the time.*

Diego: *what about me? i work an go 2 summer school.*

Ellie: *whadda tough life.*

Diego: *wanna switch? never mind. listen. i called brenda. we can go there satrday. see moochie.*

Ellie: *i might not go. i dont like how you treated me.*

Diego: *i told u thats over. i m sorry. i mean it. pleese give me another chance.*

Ellie: *have 2 think about it.*

Diego: *call u 2 morrow.*

Ellie: *ok. bye.*

Diego: *all u can say is bye. tell me u love me.*

Ellie:

Diego: *fine. be mean. tell miguel 2 b at the mart 10 30 sat morning. tell him my car has a new paint job. metallic black. red racing stripe.*

Ellie: *ok. thanks for helping miguel. he misses tae kwon do real bad n we both miss mooch real bad 2. is he ok?*

Diego: *brenda says yes so dont worry. i miss u every minute. luv u.*

Ellie: *ditto.*

BILLY: *U SAID yor on vacation. but yor dad is still home. thats different.*

Miguel: *i guess. so hows it goin?*

Billy: *dont change the subject. yor dad is lookin bad. tired and shit. whats with that?*

Miguel: *who knows? i m not home.*

Billy: *jamie said he dont come home til real late most nites.*

Miguel: *probly eats out.*

Billy: *maybe but yor mailbox is stuffed and theres newspapers on the lawn. thought he was anal.*

Miguel: *he is. i cant explain the mess.*

Billy: *get real. where r u? who r u?*

Miguel:

Billy: *this is billy. remember me? yor best friend.*
Miguel: *sorry. dont know what 2 say.*
Billy: *ttyl. maybe.*

15

AFTER CAMP FRIDAY, Ellie and I head straight for the kitchen. Mom's making supper and we're helping.

Only she's not in the kitchen.

"Uh oh," Ellie says. "Maybe she forgot."

We run upstairs. Mom's sitting at the desk. Rocking, crying, looking like someone I don't know. I think of all the bad times at home, but remember only one other time she cried like this: when her father died.

Ellie runs over. "Mom, what's wrong?"

"My life, that's what." She points to a pile of paper. "I just talked to Marsha—the legal advocate, about the next court date."

She blows her nose. "This time, we'll be in criminal court and Dad will be there. I don't know what he'll do. I'm still afraid of him, but sometimes I think it was stupid for us to come here. We have no money, most of our stuff is at home and I don't want to go there to collect it. Maybe moving out was a big mistake."

"No, it wasn't!" Ellie says and she puts her arms around Mom. Presses her face on Mom's face.

Mom shakes her head. "I don't know. I guess I'm a mess."

"We're all a mess," I say.

Under Ellie's arms, Mom's shoulder bones stick out. Her dress is too loose, her nails aren't polished, her hair is tangled.

She's not as proud of her appearance as she used to be. Dad did this to her with all his criticizing and cruelty. Sometimes I hate every molecule in his body. But sometimes I wish we could get together and kick the ball around the back yard or make hamburger runs after Tae Kwon Do.

He was so proud when I passed a promotion test. He'd go straight to the *dojang* shop before my next class and ask, "What belt should Mike wear now?"

I guess I'm like Mom. I remember mostly the good things, forget lots of the bad.

Ellie rubs Mom's shoulder. "Don't worry. We'll go to court with you, be witnesses if you need us, but please don't talk about going back home. I'll never live with Dad again, I mean it! I'll move in with Florie before I'll do that."

Mom looks shocked, then nods. "You're right. I'm sorry. I'm only thinking of myself. We can't go back."

Ellie hugs her tighter. "Thanks, Mom."

I should be mad enough at Dad to protect the girls, get revenge on him. But promise to be *a witness in court?* Tell on him, get him sent to jail?

Maybe Ellie can do that, but I'm not sure I can. Do I have to?

Mom wipes her eyes. "I know you kids think I'm crazy, but we've been married a long time. Sometimes I miss him."

Ellie sighs. "Me, too. But that doesn't change how I feel about him. He's toxic, Mom. He'll never change, but I have. I won't take his crap anymore!"

"Me, neither," Mom says. "At least that's how I *think* I feel." She pulls a card out of her purse, shows it to us. "Today Marsha told me Ron, the State Prosecutor, is going to interview both Dad and me in criminal court."

"Whose side is he on?" I ask.

"Ours. It's the State versus Dad, which is why he's hired a lawyer."

"But we have the pictures of what he did to you and Ellie, right?"

She turns around in her chair, sits up straighter. "Yes, and Marsha says I have a good case, but I keep thinking, what if I lose? He's after joint custody of you kids, not just visitation."

Something doesn't feel right about Dad's fight to get custody. He never worried much about school and doctors and family stuff before. Left all that up to Mom.

Maybe he doesn't really care about us. Maybe he just wants to force Mom to keep in touch with him through us kids. "What happens if Dad gets custody, too?" I ask.

"You kids might have to live with him half the time."

"Oh, that sounds like fun. Especially when we go back to school."

I've never been real organized, except when it came to Dad's notes. If we have to live with both Mom and Dad, we'll have to drag books, homework, sports equipment—everything, back and forth. I know what will happen. I'll forget stuff, leave things I need at the other house.

"He won't get custody, but let him try," Ellie says. "Let him waste his money." She looks at her watch. "Uh, oh. It's late. Mom, do you know you're supposed to have dinner ready in a half hour?"

"Oh, no! I totally forgot!" She jumps up and heads for the door. "Come on, we can do it."

And we did. We made spaghetti with defrosted hamburger in the sauce and salad with peaches!

"You sure came through," Keesha teased us while we ate. "I was all ready to make tomato soup and lots of grilled cheese sandwiches."

Later, Ellie and I go upstairs. She looks all excited and happy when Diego calls. Tells me after that she's "in love." I do not say Word because she's decided she will go to Brenda's on Saturday with Diego and me!

Talk about relief. Now I don't have to spend time with Diego alone. I wasn't looking forward to that.

When we get to the Mart Saturday morning, Diego's flashy car is parked out front. The minute he sees us, he jumps out and opens Ellie's door.

"What a gentleman," she gushes.

I get in back.

Dee kisses her cheek. "For you, anything."

He starts up the car, revs the engine. Asks Ellie, "Isn't Brenda's house near yours?"

She nods. Drops her head on his shoulder, sighs.

Diego groans. "Oh, man, I missed you so much." He pulls her close and kisses her long and hard.

I stare out the window. I guess this is love, but I wish they'd cool it in public.

Then Ellie starts squeaking. I look back and almost grab Diego by the hair. She has both hands on his chest, trying to push him away. He's ignoring her like she's so much meat!

She whacks his shoulder and head until he lets her go. Scoots away from him, her face and neck bright red.

"What were you thinking?" she yells. "Don't ever do that again! My brother's in the back seat! You want him giving Mom a make-out report?"

"Sure. Want a lesson little brother?" He laughs, grabs her shoulders and pulls her into another clinch. This time she yanks on his hair, but he won't let go.

Now I'm mad. I've made my moves on a couple girls. But if a girl says no, I stop. Period.

I move forward, set my fists on the front seat, every muscle on alert until I see his bulging neck and shoulders up close. He has at least forty pounds on me, mostly muscle.

Then he pins Ellie's hands and I don't care what he does to me. I half-stand, grab the driver's neck rest. Lean over and yell in his ear, "Cool it, Diego! Stop it!"

He doesn't hear a thing.

I pinch his shoulders, pull them back until his head presses hard on the head rest. I yell, "She said *no!* Cut it out!"

Might as well be talking to a brick.

I open the back door, slam it. Open his.

He finally pulls away and looks at me. Lets her go. "Yeah, yeah." Smiles and licks his lips. What a freakin' pig!

I get back in the car, leave the back door open in case Ellie decides to split. Right now, she's so mad she can't talk. Shakes her head, grabs her purse. Scoots over to her door and blurts, "I was right. You don't deserve a girl like me. See ya."

Good. I don't want to go anywhere with him, either. We can walk to Brenda's house or call her. We don't need him.

I'm about to step outside when Ellie opens her door and Diego pounds on the wheel with both fists. BAM!

We stare at him, frozen in place.

He leans over and pulls her door shut. "What is this, your time of the month? Calm down, girl! Talk about hysterical women! You know I didn't mean nothin'. I just missed you so bad and you looked so good. I couldn't help it, understand?"

I wait for fireworks. Ellie won't let him blame his crap on hormones!

She folds her arms over her chest. Looks away, says nothing. This is not the way Ellie works. When she's dissed, she fights back. Hard.

Diego stares at her like she's crazy. "What is wrong with you?"

Her voice is soft but tough. "I'm not going anywhere with someone who 'can't help' how he acts with me. Maybe you won't be able to 'help it' at Brenda's, either. You think I want her watching you maul me? You think she won't tell my mother? Maybe *I'll* tell my mother!"

I sit back, ready to leave if she does. That was a pretty good speech, but she needs to exit the car.

Diego leans toward her. His voice gets low and nasty. "Was that a *threat?* Don't dis me, girl. I'm a man. I was on fire, that's all."

"Bullshit!" she yells, doing the snaky-neck thing. "Not letting go when I punch you and tell you to stop is dissing *me!*"

That's better, girl!

He moves back a little.

"What didn't you understand about, 'Don't ever do that again?'" she asks in an icy voice.

Now she's talkin'.

Diego's shoulders slump. "Okay, okay. You're right, baby. I'm sorry." His voice is soft, silky. "I'm so sorry. You know how much I love you."

Ellie's voice is not soft. It drips with her old 'know-it-all' tone. "I guess you forgot that this is not a date. You're doing us a favor, and I appreciate that. We both want to see Moochie and Miguel wants a Tae Kwon Do lesson. That's what today is about, okay? It's not about you and me."

I'm still breathing hard. Sounds like she's giving him another chance, probably so I'll get my lesson. But I'm not sure I want one anymore. Dee's nothing like Master Han or the other teachers at my dojang. They teach "Do"—"the way" of Tae Kwon Do: self-control, unity of body and mind.

I don't see any of that in Diego. I see impulsive, mean, selfish, nasty.

"Awright," he grunts. "Let's forget about it and go to Brenda's, okay?"

I pull my door shut. Ellie turns her back to Dee and the car gets real quiet.

After a long half hour, Ellie says, "I'll tell you where to turn when we get close."

Her voice is still cold. She pretends huge interest in the apartment buildings, homes, and parks flying by. Doesn't look at Dee.

It's ugly hot again and Dee's car has no air conditioning, which is no prob for me. I'm wearing shorts and a tee shirt, but Ellie's wearing jeans. What's with that?

And then I remember. Her leg still looks scabby and the bruise hasn't faded that much.

When she tells Diego the name of Brenda's street, he says, "I thought so. Brenda's house is only five minutes from your house. Let's go say hi to your dad. He's gotta be missing you guys."

Right. We'll just swing by and spend some quality time with Dad. Pretend there's no restraining order.

Before I can open my big mouth, Ellie says in her fake-silk voice, "Why would I want to see him?" She pulls up her jean leg and shows Diego the damage.

Not pretty.

He barely glances at her leg. "Doesn't look that bad."

I want to punch his face in. What's wrong with him, acting like what Dad did is no big deal? I open my mouth to tell him how hard Dad shoved her. How hard she hit the table. How much blood and pain I saw.

He turns the radio up loud and drives way too fast.

Ellie looks away, blinks hard. Crosses her arms across her chest.

Finally Dee says, *"What?"*

She takes a deep breath. "Did you forget that Dad hurt Mom and Moochie real bad, too?"

"No, but sometimes women exaggerate..."

Ellie grabs her purse. Looks ready to slug him with it or take off when the car stops.

I settle back, wish I was somewhere else. Even the shelter. At least there aren't any rotten guys living there.

I think about staying in the car when we get to Brenda's, but she sees us pull into the driveway and opens the kitchen door. Moochie's behind her, barking nonstop.

We go inside the house. I bend down, try to pick Moochie up. He runs back and forth so fast I can't catch him. We laugh, wait for him to calm down.

All of a sudden, he whimpers. Squats next to Dee and pees a little.

"You stupid dog!" Diego screams. "You pissed on my shoe!" He grabs Mooch behind his head like he's a cat.

I can't move. He looks like he plans to rub Moochie's nose in the puddle! Maybe some people train puppies this way, but Mooch isn't a puppy. And he's never had accident one at home. I know he didn't mean to pee inside.

"Let him go," Ellie says. No silk in her voice this time. More like steel.

Diego drops Moochie and steps back. "Sorry."

He doesn't look sorry. He looks mad.

"It's my fault," Brenda says and gives Dee a wet paper towel to clean his shoe. "I should have had him pee before you got here. Just take him outside with you."

"Okay, thanks," I say and let Moochie out. He flies off the deck. Runs to the back fence. Does his business.

"See?" Ellie says. "He was just nervous and excited."

Diego snorts. "That right? Do you pee on the floor when you're nervous and excited?" He smiles. "Guess I'll have to train you."

Ellie gives him the evil eye. Calls Moochie back to the deck and holds him like a baby. Looks ready to cry.

This is no fun. "Could we start the Tae Kwon Do lesson?" I ask. I want to get it over with and get rid of Mr. Crazy.

He pulls off his tee. "Sure."

Dee's not that tall, but he has rock-hard muscles in places I didn't even know we have muscles. "Okay, show me your stuff, Miguel. Let's start with stretching and then we'll practice the *hyungs* for your next test."

We bow to each other. Work hard for a long time. He knows his stuff, at least the patterns, and he has the fitness, perseverance, and indomitable spirit you need in martial arts.

But he doesn't have the courtesy or respect Master Han says we should show others all the time. I'm not doing this with him again.

The sun feels red hot on my shoulders and head. The air feels wet. Pretty soon, I'm soaked with sweat, tired, and real thirsty.

The back door opens and Ellie comes out. She sets a tray with a tall pitcher on the deck table.

Yes! Lemonade!

"Anyone want a cool drink?" she asks.

"You read my mind." I take two steps toward her and Diego lifts me off the ground from behind. Chokes me with my own tee shirt so hard I wonder if my neck is getting sawed off. Or bleeding.

I stand on my toes, drag at his hand. "Cut it out! What are you doing?"

He doesn't loosen his grip. "Did you bow to your teacher? Did you get permission from him to leave?"

The memory of Dictator Dad at his worst rushes back. The cold, hard voice. The threat of his strength. The fury because I didn't do something exactly as he'd expected.

Ellie runs over. "Let him go, asshole!" She scores a direct kick on Diego's shinbone.

Crack.

Diego grunts, lets go of me.

"Thanks, Sis." I stumble away from Diego, stay close to Ellie. I press my fingers against my neck, front and back. No blood. Just sweat and pain in a throbbing circle.

"Let's go," Ellie says quietly. She's watching Diego like he's a mad dog.

He's hunched over, rubbing his leg, shaking his head side to side. "Son of a bitch, son of a bitch!"

We back toward the door. Moochie's barking like mad, staying close to Ellie's leg.

"Quiet," she tells him.

119

He barks louder.

We stop dead when Dee jumps up, drops his chin, and runs at us like we're tackling dummies.

I flip into Survival Mode. Look for someplace to hide.

Next to me, Ellie's breathing hard. Her face is pale, her body trembling.

Okay, hiding's out.

I check how far we are from the back door and stop moving. I don't care how strong Dee is. He's not hurting Ellie again.

"Run, get Brenda," I tell her. "Now!"

"No," she says.

I step in front of her, but we're close together, perfect targets. He'll stomp us!

"Aggression in Tae Kwon Do is for self-defense only."

I yell, "Ki-hap!" Turn sideways, my eyes locked on Dee's. I raise my hands, elbows cocked. Bend my back knee.

Ready.

Dee stops dead like someone slapped him.

Raises his hands palms out. "Okay, okay. I'm sorry. I got carried away, but how could I help it? Students don't take off during training! You treated your instructor like garbage! Tae Kwon Do is about *respect!* Did you forget that?"

My neck muscles are already tightening up. I want to ask, "What about the instructor's respect for his students? Did you forget that?"

But I don't. Waste of time. He's just like Dad, blaming me for his bad behavior. And I don't know where Diego learned Tae Kwon Do, but it sure wasn't with someone like Master Han.

Ellie scoops up Moochie. "Let's go, Miguel. Brenda can take us home." Her voice is shaky but her chin is up.

Diego nods his head like some stupid car toy. "Oh, that fits. You'll show Brenda where you live but not me, right?"

"I wouldn't get in a car with you if I had to crawl home."

"Ditto," I said.

Which was stupid. We were making Dee madder every time we spoke and that's a losing game with these guys.

I take a quick look to make sure we were headed in the right direction, just in case.

We are. Just a few more feet and we can run for the back door.

"Hey, that's okay," Dee sneers. "You're in charge, right, girl? And you're welcome for the lesson, Mike. Let's do it again sometime."

Right.

I turn my back on him and pray he won't jump me. Walk toward the house at normal speed and don't look back.

He doesn't follow us, but as soon as Ellie and I are in the kitchen, I slam the door and lock it. No sense taking chances.

When I realize what Dee could have done to Ellie and me, I gasp for air like I've been under water a long time. Don't breathe normally again until I hear his car squeal onto the street and roar away.

Ellie drops on the nearest chair, shaking so hard I'm afraid she'll slip off.

I stand at her side, press my body against hers so she won't slide to the floor.

She doesn't need any more bruises.

16

FLORIE: *GIRLFRIEND. WHERE you been?*
    Ellie: *busy. camp stuff. helping mom.*
    Florie: *my mom called yor dad last nite. said he was drunk.*
    Ellie: *he s upset.*
    Florie: *bummer. what is wrong?*
    Ellie: *everything. my familys messed up rite now. i cant talk about it.*
    Florie: *why not? i thought we were best buds.*
    Ellie: *sorry. i just cant.*
    Florie: *ok. but better call me when u can. luv u.*
    Ellie: *xo*

DIEGO: *ELLIE HAVE pity. i know yor mad about how i treeted miguel and you and moochie yesterday. but it aint gonna happen again. u gotta beleeve me.*
    Ellie:
    Diego: *i dont no why i go off like that. mayb u can help me. teach me how to control my temper. pleese. we gotta talk. anywhere u want. any time u want.*
    Ellie:

DAD: *HI ELLIE.*
    Ellie: *yor not allowed to text me. no contact. remember?*

Dad: *i have no other choice. you wont answer my calls and i cant write to you. listen. i am still your dad and i need a favor.*

Ellie:

Dad: *you there. tell mom to call me. i only want to talk and will meet her wherever she wants.*

Ellie:

Dad: *come on. i love you. you know i didn't mean to hurt you. i am so so sorry. call me, please. the court doesnt have to know.*

Ellie:

DIEGO: *HEY MR. c. hows it going?*

Dad: *not so good. my family wont talk to me. not even ellie.*

Diego: *join the club.*

Dad: *i thought you and ellie made up.*

Diego: *we did but we had another fight. she s mad at me again. wont talk. wont text.*

Dad: *same here. thats her new thing. shut us out.*

Diego: *and get this. i have 2 pick her up n drop her off at a quick mart. she wont let me pick her up at the shelter. wont even walk to the shelter til i m out of site.*

Dad: *i am not surprised. they brainwash women in that place. hang on. love will win out.*

Diego: *meanwhile i feel like shit.*

Dad: *me too. women are good at that. later.*

17

NEXT NIGHT, I'M sitting on my top bunk. Mom's asleep. Ellie's sitting on her bed, gripping her phone like it might run away. First she reads and texts. Then she only reads.

Oops. She drops the phone and starts crying. It's gotta be Diego on the line, but why is she reading his texts? I thought they were through.

She stashes her phone under the pillow and looks up at me. "Stop watching me, a-hole! I know I'm messed up. I gotta get more serious about finding a job. It'll keep my mind off Dee."

"Good idea. And when you get your first paycheck, buy a new cell phone. One he can't call."

Bad choice of words. She starts sobbing.

I jump down, sit on her bed. "Shhhh! You'll wake up Mom! Why are you crying about him? He's psycho!"

She wipes her eyes. "Maybe. I don't know. He's so upset, too upset to be nice right now. His parents are splitting and he's real sad."

"Our parents are splitting, too. Are you abusing him?"

She cries harder. "I don't know, I don't know."

Huh? She still thinks Diego's crap is her fault? What happened to my tough sister? She's as confused as Mom was a while ago. For the zillionth time, I wish I could tell Mom what's going on. Maybe she could help Ellie think straighter.

Except sometimes Mom isn't thinking that straight herself. And she doesn't need more stress.

She got Dad arrested for calling Ellie, so now she doesn't need to hire a lawyer. She and Dad will be in Criminal Court because Dad broke the restraining order. And the State Prosecutor will be on her side!

And she meets with Marsha a lot. I think that's helping her. She doesn't cry anymore but she's still tired all the time.

Ellie blows her nose. "Okay, I admit it. Dee can be a total jerk. But we used to have so much fun. I miss him. I keep hoping he'll change back to how he used to be."

"Oh. You mean the way *Dad* always changed back? The way he's Mr. Nice Guy for a few days and then gradually gets even meaner than before? You sound just like Mom used to—insane."

Her phone bounces off my shoulder.

18

DIEGO: *PLEASE TALK to me. text me. i miss u so much. i even look for u when i deliver pizzas. my boss is pissed. he says i m delivering 2 slow.*

Ellie:

Diego: *he s right. plus i skipped summer school all week. kept thinking how bad i messed up with you wen we were going to brendas house. treated u wrong in front of yor brother. i need u so bad. i cant talk to mom becuz she s mad all the time and i dont know where dad is. maybe i will never see him again.*

Ellie:

Diego: *i thot u loved me. if thats true lets try again. i know u gave me another chance already and i blew it. i swear i dont want 2 act this way. help me change so it wont happen again.*

Ellie:

Diego: *at least let me know u r ok.*

Ellie:

Diego: *dont u care?*

Ellie:

19

THE NEXT DAY, Mom and Ellie go straight to Pilar's office after camp. They don't even show up for supper, which is no loss. They don't like fish sticks and frozen fries either. I nuke a couple cheese sandwiches, inhale them and return to the room.

Ellie shows up right after I get there. She looks pretty bad. Mascara running, antsy, hair wild. Scans the room like someone might be hiding in the closet.

"What's going on?" I ask.

She plops down on the floor and sits back against her bed. Wipes her eyes and breathes deep. "Nothing. Wanna play Rummy?"

"Okay." We flop on the floor between her bed and Mom's. I deal the cards, turn over the starter. "You go first."

Just like that, she turns into Wild Woman. Tosses every discard at me like a weapon. Kisses every good card and laughs hysterically when she puts down a set.

"Geez, calm down." I pick up my discard. "Now watch carefully. Here is where you put the discards." I set my card soooo carefully on the pile.

"Yeah, yeah. You're just mad 'cause you're losing."

"Says who?"

She slams down two sets and a discard. "I'm out."

I don't shuffle the cards. She needs to talk, not play crazy girl. I sit back and give her a look.

She takes a deep breath. "Yeah, yeah. Don't say it. Mom and Pilar already let me have it for the last hour. They said what you said. I've gotta stop reading Dee's texts and listening to his messages. End of story."

"Sounds like a plan."

She shrugs. "I know. I got sucked in 'cause he left a new phone for me at the Mart. And I took it. I just wanted to hear his voice. I didn't text him back."

"If you still need him that bad, then call him, tell him you'll go out with him again. He'll be completely different, I bet. A model gentleman. Just don't tell him I want another Tae Kwon Do lesson."

She gives me the finger and grabs her purse. "Fine. Now look. I picked these up today."

She fans out applications from McDonald's and a couple other fast food joints in the neighborhood.

"Now you're cookin'. Get a job. Pay your own phone bill."

"Yeah, I know. I've gotta take care of myself, but sometimes I'm not sure I can, not alone, anyway." Tears pop out, roll down her cheeks.

I sigh and roll my eyes. Shake my head like I can't believe *her,* for a change.

"He's my friend, *estupido!* I need him," she yells. "Didn't you ever lose a friend?"

"Not like him! I wouldn't be friends with someone who treats me like dirt!" I yell back.

I can't stand it! How she can want to be with someone who's as mean as Dad?

Whoa. My turn to take a deep breath.

I've gotta remember what Pilar said. This is Ellie's problem. Her head's messed up. I can't fix it. And if I keep trying to, we'll both stay mad.

I stand up and leave the room before I do something stupid.

20

ELLIE: *GIRL.*

Florie: *what up stranger?*

Ellie: *i m looking 4 a job.*

Florie: *hey. someone just quit at the shop today. you can make sandwiches. come down and apply. it will be so fun to work together an u can sleep at my house when yor workin late.*

Ellie: *no i cant.*

Florie: *why not. come on. this is killin me. i havent seen u 4 weeks. i feel like i lost my sister.*

Ellie: *me 2 but your job is too close to my house.*

Florie: *so what?*

Ellie: *cant tell u.*

Florie: *that again.*

Ellie:

Florie: *whats goin on? we never keep secrets from each other.*

Ellie: *i know an yor right.*

Florie:

Ellie: *okay heres the story. mom and miguel and me r living in hawkinstown. in a battered womens shelter. mom got a restraining order against dad.*

Florie: *wow. didnt know he was that bad.*

Ellie: *he s worse than bad.*

Florie: *but r u comin back? i cant deal with college boards and all that alone.*

Ellie: *me neither but i m too messed up to think high school right now never mind college.*

Florie: *i feel so bad 4 u. anything i can do?*

Ellie: *yeah. keep in touch but dont tell anyone what happened.*

Florie: *i promise. at least come sleep over my house.*

Ellie: *i cant. u live too close 2 my dad. what if he saw me n made a scene at yor house?*

Florie: *then we dont let him in. we call 911.*

Ellie: *diego is looking 4 me 2.*

Florie: *so wot.? r u scared of him 2?*

Ellie: *a little. more like confused and sad.*

Florie: *girl. come see me. u can take a bus here right? mom would luv it an i wont tell her nothin. gotta go. love u.*

Ellie: *love u back.*

BILLY: *WHATS GOIN on with u? vacation dont mean no texts. no calls. no call backs.*

Miguel: *sorry. my fones still dead and its hard to borrow moms or ellies.*

Billy: *bullshit. moms get busy. sisters sleep.*

Miguel:

Billy: *fine. u want it like that. call me when yu remember whose got yor back.*

Miguel:

21

I'M BUMMED. I want to tell Billy about Dad but I'm afraid he'll tell the guys. And they'll tell the girls and then everyone will know.

Can't deal with it, even though I miss my friends. I still miss Dad once in a while, too, but not as much as I used to. I don't know if that's a good thing or not.

I've learned one thing in group, how bullies like Dad are all the same. Only I'm not going to be like them. I am never, and I mean *never* gonna treat my girl or my family like Dad does.

I am also going to learn to cook in case my wife doesn't like to, because it's fun. Right now Bev's making cheeseburgers and macaroni salad for supper, two of my favorites. The weather finally cooled off some, so some of the moms made bag suppers tonight. Took their kids to the park.

I could have gone for that, too, but Mom doesn't have time for picnics. She's working hard getting ready for court. Wants full custody of us until we're eighteen, and she's talking like she's ready to fight for it.

It feels weird, Mom planning my relationship with Dad for the next three years. I guess I don't want to see him right now, but what if I get curious before I turn eighteen? What if I want to see if a miracle happened and he's turned into a decent person?

Yeah, right. What am I worrying about? There's no chance of that happening.

I fill my plate and sit down in the dining room. A girl about eighteen walks in. She's tall and thin with wavy red hair. And wearing a brand new cast on her wrist and a dark bruise across her nose.

She sits down at the next table, facing me. Stares out the window until Bev brings her a burger. "Thanks," she says. Drops her head, eats slowly.

That's when Carter plows in, Rock Star hair flying around. He stops dead when he sees the cast. Stares at it.

What's so fascinating, Carter?

I hate looking at the cast myself because it means someone hurt her, bad. And because it reminds me of what happened to Mom.

"Get a burger," I say to distract him. "They're great."

He loads his plate with macaroni salad and his burger with ketchup. Comes back, sits next to me.

Which is weird. Why didn't he sit across from me? Does he like looking at someone who's sad and hurt?

"Hey," he says to the girl. "You're new, right? What's your name?"

She looks up slowly, mutters, "Maribel."

Rock star smile. "Hi! I'm Carter. Nice cast you got there. Your osteoporosis kickin' up?"

Her eyes narrow and she stands up. Drops her food and paper plate in the garbage.

Bev walks over, says something quietly. Maribel shakes her head, stares at Carter, and leaves.

Bev gives Carter the evil eye.

"What is wrong with you, saying something like that?" I ask loudly so she knows I'm dealing with it.

"Just teasin'," he says. Takes a big bite of burger.

I'd like to punch him or at least invent a really bad name for him, but I don't. He must have wallowed in some ugly shit to end up as mean as he is. "Right. We all tease new women at the shelter who have been beaten up." I put down my fork and lean into his face. "Who treated you bad?"

"Nobody!" He looks at me like I'm crazy.

"Then why are you and your mom here?"

He shrugs. "My stepfather's a bastard."

"Where's your dad?"

He shrugs. "I don't know. He left before the divorce was final."

"Because...?"

He stands up, throws down his fork. "What is this, an interrogation?"

"Sit," I say, soft but firm. "Give me five minutes."

He sits. We talk. Bev's kids show up so we go to the living room and talk some more. Decide our homes aren't that different and our dads aren't either. He loses the Macho stuff, the sneer, the fake cool. But not his lousy philosophy about men having it all over women.

"You ever do any martial arts?" I ask him.

"No."

"Want to?"

He nods. "I could go for that."

"Fine. I can teach you what I've learned. In the back yard. How's tomorrow night after supper?"

He looks surprised. "Really? You'd do that for me?"

"Sure, as long as you don't keep going after women in pain."

He looks away. "It's a habit."

I use my cold voice. "Yeah? Then break it."

He nods. "I'll try. You said tomorrow after supper?"

"Yeah, I'll be there."

"Thanks." He walks through the dining room to the hall. His head is down, his steps slower.

Bev stares at him, raises her eyebrows at me after he leaves.

I shrug. "We talked, but whether he'll change his lousy attitude..."

"You never know," she says. "Look how confused you were when you came."

"Yeah, and sometimes I still am."

She smiles and waves toward the breakfast bar. "Too confused for chocolate cake?"

"Never!" I say and cut myself a big piece.

Another new woman walks in. She's young and tiny like Ellie. Carries a little boy on her hip. He's maybe three and speaking baby Spanish.

Bev fills a plate, grabs a smaller plate and two forks. Offers them to the woman.

"Thanks," she says and they sit down across from me.

The woman smiles, says, "Hi. I'm Felicia and this is Frankie."

I smile back. "I'm Mike. Hey, little guy." Frankie hides his face in Felicia's arm. No smile.

"That's okay," I say. "I guess you're shy."

Felicia looks sad. "No, he's afraid of men."

She puts some small pieces of hamburger and a little macaroni salad on Frankie's plate. He holds a fork, but eats with his fingers. Keeps his head down unless his mother talks to him.

I pull out a couple hard candies, show them to Felicia. "Can I give him these?"

You don't feed shelter kids without their mom's permission.

She nods. "Sure."

I ask Frankie, "You like candy?" in Spanish. Push the pieces toward him.

"Grathi," he says so soft I can hardly hear him. He drops his fork and grabs one. Opens it like a pro. No smile but glances my way.

"Enjoy," I say in Spanish. "Candy is fun food."

Dad says we should speak English all the time. But he didn't count on my running into a scared baby who only speaks Spanish.

I guess Dad can't think of everything. Not that he'd admit it.

After I watch a one-star movie, I go upstairs. Kick off my shoes and crash on the top bunk. Think about me when I was three. Was I afraid of men? Was Dad so mean and controlling then?

Why can't I remember?

Mom's the first one asleep, as usual, and Ellie's texting in the dark. And giggling.

I whisper, "What's so funny, Ell?"

She whispers back, "Diego's taking me to a rock and roll show tomorrow night. Stars from the fifties and sixties."

"Huh? I thought Mom said you couldn't go out with him."

"I know, but we talked a long time on the phone today. He's changed. He's nicer and more relaxed. More like he used to be."

"So was Dad, after he hurt Mom real bad."

"Diego is not Dad!"

"Oh, right. I forgot. He's a nice guy."

Silence.

Finally she says, "I don't care what you think. I'm going out with him, but don't tell Mom. She thinks I'm going to Florie's for a sleep over. She doesn't need to know Diego's picking me up there before supper."

"But what if he gets nasty again? I don't have a phone anymore. You can't call me. "

"No need! I'll be fine."

I remember Dee grinding his face into hers in the car. Treating her like his toy. How could she trust him after that?

Talk about a short memory. I should tell Mom about this date, but if I do, Ellie will never tell me anything again. And that's even more dangerous.

So I lie here, scared and shaking inside. I feel like I'm trapped in a ravine with a wild river rushing straight for me. I have no place to run and no place to hide.

So I wait for a miracle.

22

ELLIE: *HEY.*

Florie: *girl. how u doin?*

Ellie: *good. dee and i made up. he s taking me to the rockin oldies show.*

Florie: *i told u he s fine. wish hector was like him. our dates are so bor...ring.*

Ellie: *dont knock it. exciting can be scary.*

Florie: *i wouldnt know.*

Ellie: *btw i might have a job at mcdonalds. and its only a five minute walk so no bus fare.*

Florie: *beats my job.*

Ellie: *i need a favor tho. can i sleep over your house tomorrow. r curfew is so early i would miss half the show.*

Florie: *sure. mom has girls nite out fridays. she wont know if u come back late.*

Ellie: *great. just dont tell her about my date ok? moms mad at dee. said we cant go out.*

Florie: *huh?*

Ellie: *will tell u tomorrow. cover 4 me ok? i m catching a different bus from camp so its a short walk to yor house.*

Florie: *good. so heres what i tell mom. yor coming here straight from camp. going to the mall with me and sleeping over.*

Ellie: *perfect. thanks girlfriend. see u around 4 or so.*

DAD: *HAVEN'T HEARD from you lately. whats going on?*

Diego: *me and Ellie made up. goin out 2 nite. dinner and a show.*

Dad: *good for you. hey what time you dropping her at the mart? maybe i can follow her to the shelter.*

Diego: *not tonite. she s sleeping at a friends house n catchin a bus back to the city in the a.m. i dont know when.*

Dad: *so offer to pick her up.*

Diego: *i better not push it. its our first date in a while. dont want her mad at me again.*

Dad: *yor right. and if she catches me following her she might turn me in 4 violating the order.*

Diego: *that is so wrong. what happened 2 yor rights? judges shouldnt take kids away after only hearing one side.*

Dad: *yor a smart kid, Diego. keep in touch.*

23

AFTER CAMP THE next day, I start to board our bus.

Oops! Ellie's taking a different bus tonight and I gotta give her something before she leaves.

I go up a couple steps and look around the bus. Only five, six kids so far. I've got time to talk to her.

"Gotta give my sister something. Be right back," I promise the driver.

"Okay, but make it quick."

I hit the ground and Ellie runs by! Big smile, waves. "See ya tomorrow, Miguel!"

I don't smile back. She's going out with Psycho tonight. Alone. She thinks everything will be wonderful. She thinks she's got her old boyfriend back.

Sure she does. Until he changes.

I chase her, grab her arm. "Hold on!" Give her a small piece of paper. "You might need this."

She looks at it, whispers, "Is this the Hotline number? I don't need it!"

"Just take it, okay? In case Diego goes off on ya."

She rolls her eyes, slips the paper in her wallet. "Thanks, but you're worrying for nothing. He doesn't even bug me for our address anymore. Besides, I can't call the shelter!"

"Why not?"

She looks around. "Because I lied to Mom, remember? She thinks I'll be at the mall with Florie."

"Oh, yeah. Okay, how about Florie—is she on your speed dial?"

"Sure. If there's any trouble—and there won't be, she or her dad will help me. Or I'll call 911." She taps her foot. "Do I have your permission to leave now?"

Do I have a choice?

I picture Diego going off on her for no good reason. Grabbing her phone. Smashing it, tossing it out the car window before she can make a call. What if he gets so out of control he hurts her like he hurt me?

What scares me is that lately he's been acting more and more like Dad. Blows up over nothing. Ellie does some little thing he doesn't like and he delivers big abuse. Then he butters her up and she forgets and forgives.

What is she thinking?

But there's nothing I can do.

"Yeah, sure, get going, Sis. Tell Florie I said, 'Hey', all right? And be careful!"

The bus driver yells, "Mike, let's go!"

Ellie runs to her bus. From the back she looks twelve years old. No match for Psycho. Come to think of it, I'm six inches taller than she is and I'm no match for him, either!

I flop down behind the driver. Hope Mom gets back from work early.

Not that I want to see her. One look at my face and she'll know I'm a wreck. She'll ask if I'm okay and I'll probably spill the whole date-with-Psycho thing.

The bus stops at the Mart. I jump off, coughing from its diesel fumes until halfway to the shelter. By the time I get there, I'm sweaty, hungry, thirsty, and so scared from thinking what Diego could do to my sister.

I punch in my code and step into the foyer but I don't feel safe because I don't think Ellie's safe.

I feel like I'm still outside the shelter watching Ellie twirl along the edge of the roof. She moves gracefully, quickly, confidently—like she's sure she won't fall.

But one shoe is untied.

I sign in, go straight to the bathroom and soak my head under the faucet. Drink water until my stomach hurts.

In the kitchen, Keesh is cooking supper. In the dining and living rooms, the women are talking, planning, and watching a video. The kids are playing and yelling, waiting to eat.

I walk around the first floor, check the office.

No Mom. Maybe she had to work late.

In the kitchen, Keesh is slicing hot dogs into boxed mac n' cheese. Sounds gross but tastes good if you submerge it in ketchup.

"Want me to tear up lettuce for the salad?" I ask her.

Keesh doesn't look at me. "No. I done that, but I sure could use help cleanin' up the dishes and pans."

She dumps supper into a big bowl, hands me another bowl full of salad and I grab the salad dressing. We drop everything on the breakfast bar and Keesh calls, "Supper's ready!"

I look at the clock. It's getting late. Maybe Mom's upstairs, though she usually comes down for supper by now. I'll check our room after I dry the pans.

I'm too nervous to watch what I'm doing, though. Clean up so fast, Keesh raises an eyebrow. "Mike, you workin' like the devil at your heels. What up?"

Butterflies play soccer in my stomach. "I'm wondering why Mom isn't here. She's usually back by now. You hear from her or do you know if she went upstairs?"

"Maybe the traffic is bad."

That's no answer. What's she hiding from me?

I dry the dishes and put them away. Feel so antsy I'd go for a run except I'm starving and supper smells good. Maybe Mom's just shopping or something.

Keesh and Felicia fill plates with food. Call their kids, pour milk or juice into cups. Grab some napkins.

"Hey, Keesh! Good food," Felicia says. "How about we trade jobs tomorrow? You cook supper and I will wash the floors!"

Keesh smiles. "Girl, you got a deal!"

I fill my plate, eat fast. Keesh sits down across from me.

"This is good, Keesh. Thanks."

"You're welcome." She's still not looking at me. Not eating much, either.

I try again. "Keesh, you got any idea why Mom's so late?"

"Yeah," she says, "But she better tell you. She'll be home soon."

"But she's almost two hours late! I need to know if she's all right. Please."

She sighs. "Okay. She called me from work, right before you got back from camp."

I stare at her.

"Why didn't you tell me?" I yell. "If there's a problem, I have a right to know!"

"She say *don't* tell you."

I jump up. "I don't care what she said! Is she okay? Should I call 911?"

Keesh slides her chair a couple feet back from the table. "She already called 911."

"Why? What happened? Come on, give!"

Keesh is gripping the sides of her chair like it might levitate, but at least she's looking at me.

"Your mother's at the police station because your dad showed up at her job and made trouble."

"That just shows you what a dope he is. He's got a restraining order, and he's going to court already."

"Yeah. He don't play by the rules," Keesh said. "These guys think the rules not made for them."

I nod and look away. Bev, Kobi and Kojo are walking toward us, slowly. And they look scared.

What's going on?

Then I get it, and I'm ashamed. I'm acting mean, and I got too loud. They're afraid I'll hurt Keesh!

I sit down, blink hard. "I'm sorry I lost it, Keesh. I'm not mad at you, and I would never hurt you. I'm just scared for my mom."

She takes a deep breath. "I know, but that ain't no excuse for you to yell around here. I understand why you were upset, but I don't like your attitude."

I look at Bev and her little boys. "I'm really sorry I lost it. Mom's always home by now. I got scared and acted stupid."

Bev nods. "I've been there, but next time, think first, okay? Talk to us! It's not like we're the enemy."

"I know. I'm sorry. I won't do that again."

But maybe I will. I remember what Ellie said about Dad's promises, how he never keeps them. Why should these women believe I'm any different from their own nasty guys?

My promises have to be better than Dad's. I have to mean them. I have to keep them.

But can I? I'm still messed up, still act like him when I'm upset. I controlled my temper at home because I was afraid of him, but I don't have him threatening me anymore.

And that's no excuse for treating women or anyone else like shit. I'm not doing it again.

Not *ever*.

From now on, I've gotta watch my temper. I've gotta shut up, walk away, *whatever* when I'm mad. Mad doesn't give me special rights to hurt others. Master Han wouldn't do that.

I look at the clock and put my head on the table. It's almost curfew, so I can't leave the shelter. I can't help Mom no matter what's going on.

And Ellie's out with Psycho.

Dad might as well be standing over me with his fist raised.

He's still in charge.

24

MOM: U PICKED *a bad day 2 call in sick. r u ok?*

Brenda: *yeah. i just had two dr. appointments. my boss rhoda called me. said robert showed up and got arrested. do u need to stay at my house cuz of curfew?*

Mom: *no but thanx. the shelter knows i m at the police station and have to sign a statement.*

Brenda: *at least he s in jail.*

Mom: *yeah but not for long. his friend will bail him out. he s shook up tho.*

Brenda: *what happened?*

Mom: *he parked out front today. watched the door all afternoon.*

Brenda: *so much for restraining orders.*

Mom: *yeah. i got so many hang ups that rhoda noticed. asked whats going on? turns out her sister had the same problem. she told me 2 call the police.*

Brenda: *good idea.*

Mom: *except i didnt. i thought he d get bored and leave.*

Brenda: *but he didnt.*

Mom: *no. at 4 he called and stayed on the line. got so nasty i sent the call 2 rhoda s line. she put him on speakerphone and heard the threats.*

Brenda: *wow.*

Mom: *yeah. she says the police can do more now she s my witness and we recorded the call.*

Brenda: *glad she was there.*

Mom: *me 2. they arrested him for violating the order. threatening and harassing me.*

Brenda: *do the kids know?*

Mom: *ellie doesnt. she s on a sleepover. miguel is real upset.*

Brenda: *poor kid. i got you all in my prayers.*

Mom: *thanks. we need them, esp me. sometimes i want 2 quit the whole fight and go home.*

Brenda: *dont even think about it. yor doing the right thing.*

Mom: *keep telling me that. i need the reminder. see ya soon.*

DIEGO: *GIRL. U looked so buetiful 2nite. we belong together.*

Ellie: *yeah. it was fun. thanks.*

Diego: *btw i need flories number. in case your fone s turned off.*

Ellie: *sure. same as mine but ends 9409.*

Diego: *thanks. starting 2 morrow let s go out every nite. i can find another job. get off by seven.*

Ellie: *dont do that ok? i m working nites when school starts.*

Diego: *so change yor hours.*

Ellie: *i cant. the only hours they can give me are 5-9.*

Diego: *how come yor putting yor job ahead of me?*

Ellie: *becuz i need school clothes and lunch money.*

Diego: *thats cold. u know I can give you any money u need. u need to quit. think about it. i will call later.*

Ellie: *no. call me tomorrow. i m 2 tired 2 talk anymore.*

Diego: *u better think about what i said.*

Ellie: *why? i like my job and i need money. my own money.*

Diego: *wrong answer. u got one hour to think it over. ttyl*

DIEGO: *HI BEAUTIFUL. hope you changed your mind about work.*

Ellie:

Diego: *you better not be stonewallin me.*

Ellie:

DIEGO: *HEY FLORIE. put ellie on the fone ok?*

Florie: *cant. she s sound asleep.*

Diego: *wake her up aw rite.*

Florie: *no way. she was so tired she fell asleep half dressed and she s gotta be at work at 7 a.m.*

Diego: *just do it. i need 2 talk 2 her.*

Florie: *then call her 2 morrow.*

Diego: *whats with u? u got your own thing going with her?*

Florie: *goodbye a hole.*

Diego: *dont hang up on me if u know whats good 4 u.*

Florie:

DIEGO: *SORRY I went off on u before. i know u and hector are tite.*

Florie: *look its one a.m. i m goin 2 bed. dont call again ok?*

Diego: *i wont if you tell ellie i gotta talk to her.*

Florie: *dont worry. i will tell her plenty—2 morrow.*

Diego: *what is wrong with u girl? just tell her i called. say more than that and u better watch your back.*

Florie: *if thats a threat thanks for the ammo. did u know threatening is a crime?*

Diego:

DIEGO: *ELLIE WHATS up with your friend? the bitch is so nasty. wont let me talk 2 u. call me as soon as u wake up. luv u.*

Ellie:

DIEGO: *ITS 6 15 am. u gotta be awake now if u work at 7. how come no call. dont believe one word florie says. she aint yor friend. came on 2 me hot n heavy last nite. but i dont want her. i want u. i have a test 2 day but call me anytime. love u always.*

Ellie:

Diego: *you there?*

Ellie:

Diego: *fine. its hardball time girl becuz yor pissin me off. now i m gonna find u. i saw a mcdonalds near the mart. bet thats where u work. i will drop in today if u don't call me by noon.*

Ellie: *last nite i thought u had changed but u havent. we r through. i dont want to date u or see u ever again. i m getting a new fone so dont call. and dont harass me at work or i will get a restraining order against u.*

Diego: *who r u? is there some other girl in yor body? time for u to see a shrink cuz yor talkin crazy. i know u love me and u belong 2 me. only me. see u soon.*

Ellie:

ल   ल   ल

DIEGO: *HEY MR C. i m in the doghouse again. ellie wouldnt call me back after r date becuz i said stupid things. she says we r thru but i know she still loves me. i think i know where she works. gonna pay her a visit.*

Dad: *i m like you. have to finish things with my wife too. make sure she goes along with me. but sometimes that gets me in trouble. maybe you better hold off. let ellie cool down.*

Diego: *its so hard to do that. i miss her so much.*

Dad: *maybe we could work together. i just traded in my truck. got a small white one.*

Diego: *wow. good move. they won't know its yors.*

Dad: *right. maybe we can take turns driving the new truck near the mart. one of us is sure to see them.*

Diego: *just say the word and i will go lookin 4 them.*

Dad: *ok. word. come to my house tonite at seven so we can talk.*

Diego: *u got it.*

BILLY: *JUST SO u know. i signed up at yor dojang. am doing good. master han says he misses you. he hopes yor all rite? r u all rite? i dont know wot to tell him.*

Miguel:

MIGUEL: *YOU SAID we can email or call u if we have a big problem.*

Master Han: *yes certainly. what is wrong? we not see you for long time.*

Miguel: *my father hurt my mother and sister. we had to move to a secret place. I can't go to yor dojang anymore. i feel very bad about that.*

Master Han: *i do too. so sorry. you are good student. work hard. live the right way.*

Miguel: *thank u. i miss u and i remember yor lessons. maybe someday i can come back.*

Master Han: *i hope so. let me know how you are. I will pray for you and your family. goodbye and good luck.*

Miguel: *thank you. for everything.*

25

SURPRISE! SUNDAY AFTER breakfast, Mom says, "No church today, kids. We're having a picnic with Brenda and Moochie at our usual spot."

"At the park?" Ellie asks. "Great! I'm dying to see Moochie again."

"Me, too," I say. "Thanks, Mom!"

"And look at this," she says.

We follow her to the fridge. She pulls a big brown package out. On it she's scribbled MERCEDES CASTILLO in black marker. "Check it out," she says and we rip it open. It's full of food we haven't had for a while.

"Yeah, gazpacho," I say. "And rice with pigeon peas. When'd you make this stuff?"

Mom laughs. "I didn't. I bought it at the Spanish market yesterday."

"Fine with me," Ellie says. "And look—mangos, rolls, and our favorite hot dogs!"

I'm practically drooling. "And salsa and chips! Wow. Great picnic, Mom."

"Thank you. There's also soda in the car and Brenda's bringing dessert."

"Okay! I'll get the ice!"

I grab an old cooler in the pantry, open the freezer and empty the ice cube trays. Ellie, my compulsive sister, immediately fills them with water again.

I give her the raised eyebrow.

"Hey, nice guy, other people might want ice cubes, too!"

"Yeah, okay. You're right." Sometimes I need her reminders not to be selfish. It's another trait of Dad's I don't want to have.

An hour later, we pull into the mart. Mom pumps gas, frowns at the price. She's trying to put most of her paycheck away for an apartment. The landlord might want the first and last month's rent, plus a safety deposit. Adds up to lots of money and she's not about to ask Dad for some.

Ellie taps her fingers on the dashboard while we wait. Looks at every car in the parking lot.

"Don't worry. No Dad or Diego." I say. "I already checked."

"I hope you're right," she says, but keeps looking around.

By the time we reach the park, I'm sweating big time. The AC in Mom's car is shot and it's another hot, humid day in Connecticut.

I don't complain. The sky is blue and the picnic food is great. Mom can't control the weather, even if Dad might try to blame it on her if he was in the car.

I need to stop thinking about him. He's out of my life now and he's going to stay out of my life.

I hope.

When we stop at our favorite picnic area, I check the cars near it. Still no bad guys.

It's not that early, so we're lucky no one has claimed our spot yet. "Not many people or cars today," I say.

"They're probably over at the pool," Mom says.

Ellie shrugs. "Yeah, but since dogs aren't allowed at the pool, I'll be happy to stay right here with Moochie!"

"Ditto," I say.

We park on the road across from our spot. There are two tables and grills under tall trees. It's quiet and shady. Best place to be on a day like this.

I watch the road. A couple 4 by 4's drive by, then a small white truck, an upscale station wagon, and a couple wrecks. But no Dad or Diego.

Guess I need to lose the paranoia. Dad's been here with us plenty of times. But he doesn't know we're here today. I need to calm down, stop looking for trouble.

I set the cooler on a table. Pop an orange soda to quiet my growling stomach.

That's when Brenda shows up. Moochie flies out of her car and I forget food. He's already seen us and is straining against the leash. He jumps, twirls, does his happy bark.

I run to the car, pick him up and hold him against my chest. He licks my face and wiggles like a puppy. I feel five years old and laugh like a nut. Rub noses and kiss him.

"Wish I could sneak you in our room," I say. I've missed him so much.

Ellie grabs him. "Yeah, but you better not, Miguel or we won't have a room!"

She holds Moochie like a baby while Mom kisses his curly little head and says, "I can't wait to get you back, little guy."

Brenda pulls two grocery bags out of her trunk. "I don't blame you. He is one sweetheart. I'm gonna miss him like crazy when he's gone. Do I get visiting rights?"

Mom smiles. "Anytime, girlfriend. Don't know what we'd have done without your help."

Ellie sets Moochie on the ground. "We'd better see if he needs to go."

We all laugh when he pulls her straight to a tree.

The Girls unpack and Moochie paces back and forth, so excited he doesn't know who he wants to be with. He heads for our heels, licks any bare skin he can reach and takes off.

I don't pick him up so he can run off his excitement. Then he'll be so sweet to hold.

"This is one beautiful place for a picnic," Brenda says.

Mom nods. "Yeah, we've always come here." She looks a little sad, and I know why. This was her favorite spot to come with Dad, before they even had kids.

The ground slopes up from the picnic area to an open field. Dad, Ellie, and I used to go up there and play softball after we ate. It was fun because Dad pitched easy to us so we could hit the ball almost every time.

I push the memory away. Don't want to get sucked into missing him again. Or forgetting why I don't miss him much anymore.

Ellie lights the charcoal while Brenda and Mom set up lunch. They blabber away and laugh a lot. It feels so good to be here until Moochie starts barking. And it's not his happy bark, either.

The Girls look up, stare at the road, stop talking.

I whip around and see good ole Diego stepping off the road and onto the grass. My heart beats faster even though he's smiling as he heads our way. What's he doing here? And where's his car?

As usual, he's dressed in black with muscles bulging everywhere. And he's carrying flowers!

I grab Moochie and hold him close. Feel him tremble.

"Are we lucky, or what?" Mom mutters and throws the meat back in the cooler.

Damn. My stomach's growling again.

"What do you want?" Mom asks Diego. She's not smiling.

None of us are.

He frowns. "Is that a friendly way to talk, Mrs. Castillo? Come on, it's a public park. I was going fishing in the pond down the road, just happened to see your car."

"And just happened to have flowers?" I ask.

"Yeah, as a matter of fact!" Diego yells.

He looks away, takes a deep breath. When he looks back, he's smiling again. He must have remembered he's supposed to be Mr. Nice Guy.

He steps a little closer, holds the bouquet out to Ellie. "This is for you, beautiful."

"No thanks," she says.

She moves away from him and close to Mom. We're all standing near the grill now. And we're making sure to keep the picnic table between Diego and us.

"What's going on, baby girl?" Diego whines. "I just wanted to see you. I've missed you so much."

Mom says, "You heard her. Go do your fishing and leave us alone. Ellie isn't allowed to see you anymore. You know that."

"She's sixteen, Mrs. Castillo. Shouldn't that be her decision?"

He's being polite, but he's not fooling me. He smiled at our house when Dad said Mom couldn't make decisions about us and now he's willing to let Ellie make decisions? What a hypocrite!

Ellie lifts her chin. Her eyes flash like the old days. She looks a little tough and real sure of herself.

I love it.

"Dee, just leave, okay?" she says. "I don't want you here, and I don't want your flowers. I told you. We're *done.*"

"You heard her," Mom says. "I guess she's made her decision."

Her voice is as icy as Ellie's. I love that, too.

It comes to me what's wrong with Dee's story. First, no fishing pole in sight. Second, I've been watching the road since we got here and never saw his hotshot car.

I look up and down the road. There's some cars near the Porta-Potties. Maybe he parked down there. I hate to leave the Girls, even for a couple minutes, but I've got to find his car.

Or not.

My stomach ices over. What if Dad drove him here?

Now I'm scared. I don't want to run into Dad. I haven't seen his blue truck, either, so I need to look for that, too. Gotta find out if he's helping Diego.

OMG. What if they're working together? Now I feel a little sick.

It's easy to look distressed with all that's going through my mind. "Sorry, Mom, but I gotta go, *bad.*"

Brenda takes Moochie, slips the leash on him again. Keeps her eyes on Dee, points with her head. "I saw some Porta-Potties down the road."

I take off running. Check out every vehicle on the way. Don't see Diego's car or Dad's truck. Maybe Dee parked near the pond and walked back, assuming his story isn't entirely bullshit.

Which it must be. If he's here to fish, and the pond's nowhere in sight, what's he doing way over here?

Then I remember Big Mouth Ellie. Maybe she told him about this spot and how Sunday's our favorite day to picnic. Maybe he took a chance she'd be here and bought flowers.

I look in every vehicle I pass in case Dee borrowed one. Don't see a single fishing pole.

I walk back fast, stay in the shade. Sweat buckets anyway. I'm too mad to be hungry any more. I just hope Diego's gone.

Diego!

What was I thinking, leaving the Girls with him? The Psycho might still be bugging them or getting physical, and I'm taking my time here!

I run flat out. Am panting when I reach our spot. Diego's standing closer to the Girls, trying to give Ellie a phone. She's pushing it away. Yelling at him, neck snaky.

Mom and Brenda are standing behind Ellie. Mom's holding a big bar-b-que fork. Could double for a weapon, it's so big.

Great, I'm thinking crazy again.

I check out the picnic. No change. The briquettes are white-hot, the grill empty. Brenda's chocolate cake is on the table. Only difference? Diego's flowers are on the ground.

"Come on, Ell," he's begging. "Just one short ride, so we can talk."

"No! Go away!"

Brenda sees me, pulls out her phone. "Time to call 911, people."

Dee laughs. "Go ahead, ladies. I'm not threatening you and it's a public park."

"Diego, forget it," I say. "Just leave, okay?"

He sneers, "You gonna make me, baby cakes?"

Ellie rolls her eyes. "Look, asshole. Mom and Brenda know you hurt Miguel and threatened Florie. And now you're harassing us and stalking me, which is illegal! You need to leave. I wasn't kidding about a restraining order and I will tell the cops the whole story. And I mean *everything*."

Diego's mouth drops open. His head shakes back and forth. He holds his hands palms up.

"Baby, how can you treat me like this? You know I love you and I'd never hurt you."

He grabs Ellie's hand.

She yanks it back.

I step between them. Lord, please don't let him punch me. "Come on, Dee. Forget it, *go*."

He makes kissing sounds. "Or else you'll what?"

"You sure you want to find out?" I ask. I don't know what level Tae Kwon Do belt he has, but muscles aren't everything in that sport.

"Oh. I am so scared," he says, but the sneer is gone.

"911?" Brenda says really loud. "I'm at the park with some friends and this guy is harassing us." She gives her name and our location.

Diego shrugs. "They won't do anything. I don't have a record. Shit, I don't even have a parking ticket!"

"Yes," Brenda says, "We know him. He injured Miguel's neck last Saturday. We have pictures."

Diego snorts. "So what? You can't prove I did that."

"Right," Mom says. "We only have three witnesses."

Diego walks over to Mom, leans into her face. Talks soft. He's doing a pretty good imitation of Dad or maybe *his* dad. I'd be scared shitless if I weren't so freakin' mad.

I move closer until I'm standing right behind him. He'd better not touch my mother.

"You don't want to make trouble for me, *Mercedes*," he says. "I got *connections.*"

Brenda holds up her phone. "Talk louder, Diego so 911 can hear your threats."

"Dee, it's time to go," I say. "She's not kidding."

He turns around, looks me up and down. A tiger discovering its prey.

The safety plans from group at the shelter race through my mind: *Stay calm. Hide if you can. Protect yourself and others if possible. Try to get help.*

A police cruiser crawls by. Diego's eyes shoot a warning at me. He turns toward the road. Smiles at the officers in the car. They look at him, keep going.

That does it. He's played us for stupid long enough. "Be right back. I'll see what the cops can do for us."

Dee looks furious, hesitates, then takes off up the hill.

I don't take any chances. Jog past the table and head for the road. Look back.

He's almost to the top of the hill. Doesn't look back. Punches a tree, keeps going.

"It's okay," Mom says as soon as he disappears. She collapses on the table bench. "Whew. Thanks, guys."

I'm shaking. We're all shaking. But we get it. We won!

Brenda smiles. "You know what? I didn't even have 911 on the line."

We all laugh and Ellie says, "Girl, you deserve an Oscar!"

Mom stands up and pulls the hot dogs out of the cooler. "No way we could have done this a month ago."

"Yeah, think about it," Ellie says. "Tough guy shows up, threatens us, acts out. We don't run or hide or give in and he *leaves!* We got what *we* wanted for a change."

My heart does its hard pounding thing but I'm not scared. More like proud.

Chalk one up for the good guys, and that includes me.

26

ELLIE: *HEY. I borrowed a fone so i could tell u i dumped dee.*

Florie: *big deal. u been mad at him b 4. next week you'll tell me you're all in love with him again.*

Ellie: *not gonna happen becuz now i hate him. if u think he s so fine. he s yours.*

Florie: *for real. what happened?*

Ellie: *he crashed r picnic today. wouldnt leave.*

Florie: *tell me all.*

Ellie: *i cant. i m late 4 work. how about a sleepover tomorrow?*

Florie: *sure. come 4 supper. do u need cash for a new fone?*

Ellie: *no thanks. moms buying one on payday.*

Florie: *thats good. no more calls from diego.*

Ellie: *or dad. see ya soon.*

Florie: *cant wait.*

DIEGO: *YOU CALLED that one rite. they were all at the park with brenda and the dog.*

Dad: *did they notice the truck?*

Diego: *i doubt it. i parked way down the road.*

Dad: *good work.*

Diego: *not that good. i walked back and asked ellie to go for a ride. she refused to come with me and i lost it.*

Dad: *you didnt hurt her right? dont hurt my daughter. u could get arrested and get me in trouble at the same time.*

Diego: *don't worry about it. i couldnt get near her.*

Dad: *so whats the problem?*

Diego: *your wife told me to leave but i didnt til mike almost flagged down a cruiser.*

Dad: *oh great.*

Diego: *dont worry. i left b 4 he got their attenshun.*

Dad: *listen up. i dont need trouble with the cops right now. if you get caught i get caught.*

Diego: *no way. i would never turn u in. but i can't live like this. i gotta know what ellies doing. what if she goes out with another guy?*

Dad: *it could happen but probly wont. women get mad but they forgive and forget. they need us. just ignore her for a while. she will call you.*

Diego: *what if they move and i lose ellie forever?*

Dad: *thats why you need to find out where they are asap.*

Diego: *got an idea. i could buy ellie a nice necklace. surprise her at work.*

Dad: *not a good idea. dont go near her job. i m telling you.*

Diego: *dont worry. i will b careful.*

Dad: *i said dont bug her. this is her father talking. you hear me?*

Diego: *yeah but i m so messed up without her.*

Dad: *you think i am having it easy with the kids and mercedes gone? but we have to play it cool. stay away till the heat's off. i mean it.*

Diego:

Dad: *i will call you after court. i have a good lawyer, should get off with a fine. meanwhile dont hassle ellie.*

Diego: *gotta go. i m working.*

Dad: *keep me in the loop.*

27

THE COURT BUILDING is brick and feels unfriendly with its closed windows and automatic shades turned against the sun.

"You kids look great," Mom says after we park. "You'll make a good impression on the judge if you have to testify."

Testify?

I hope not. I don't want to face lawyers asking a zillion questions. Making me tell everyone how bad my father is.

Especially when he's sitting right in front of me!

We follow Mom into the courthouse, go through Security. Take the elevator to the second floor and find our courtroom.

"Let's wait for Marsha," Mom says. She's pulled her curls into a fancy bun on the back of her neck and is wearing a nice pants suit. Almost looks like a lawyer herself.

We sit on a bench outside the courtroom. I hope we don't have to wait long. Just makes me more nervous.

A minute later, Mom smiles. "Here she is."

I was expecting the tough advocate Mom told me about, but Marsha is small and pretty. Has a nice smile. The tall guy with her wears a tie and a good suit. Has blonde, frizzy hair and blue eyes that go right through you.

Hope he's on our side.

"Hi, Mercedes," Marsha says. "This is Ron Fielding, the State Prosecutor." She introduces him to all of us.

He shakes our hands, says, "I'm sorry we couldn't meet before now, Mercedes, but Marsha's been filling me in on your situation. Let's find a place to talk."

The small conference room down the hall has dingy white walls, industrial carpet, one table, and six chairs. But it's private.

Ron asks a lot of questions, takes a lot of notes. "The best thing about this case right now," he says, "is that your Dad agreed to trial by judge. His lawyer got him a decent plea bargain, but a judge is better for you than a jury trial. He knows he'll get a big fine for violating the Restraining Orders and that jury trials take much longer and are much more expensive."

He pulls out pictures of Mom's and Ellie's injuries, gives each of us a paper.

"This document says Miguel and Ellie swear these pictures show the injuries their father inflicted on their mother, Ellie, and your dog, Moochie the day before you entered the shelter. And that they *witnessed* him inflicting these injuries."

He gives Ellie and me a pen. "I want everyone to read these statements carefully. Tell me if you think something needs to be added or deleted. Ellie and Miguel, if you agree with these statements, sign your copies. If you don't understand something, ask me."

"This might save you from having to testify," Marsha says.

I couldn't read the thing or sign it fast enough. I knew I'd completely choke trying to talk in front of a judge. And strangers, other lawyers, and Dad.

Especially Dad.

"You have a good case, Mercedes," Ron says after Ellie and I sign. He fans out the pictures and more signed statements from Brenda, Marsha, and Mom's boss, Rhoda. "You have several witnesses and they're all willing to testify."

He slides everything back in his briefcase, asks, "Okay, are you ready?"

Mom's voice quavers. "Not really. I don't know what Robert will do when he hears all this, especially when he hears what I have to say."

That's how scared she is, called him by his Americanized name.

Scary memories suck away my confidence, too. Dad is not Diego. He won't back off at the first sign of trouble.

Marsha pats Mom's arm. "Don't worry, Mercedes. There are Marshals here, Security."

"I know. And maybe he won't do anything today, but..." She takes a deep breath, closes her eyes.

I'm with her. Unless you live with a someone like Dad, you don't know what these guys are like or what extremes they'll go to, to get their way.

"I know things could get worse because you decided to leave Roberto," Ron says. "But we have to deal with what he has already done. Right now, he's facing possible jail time and a big fine."

He ticks Dad's crimes off on his fingers. "For the assaults at home, threatening and harassing Mercedes at work and calling Mercedes and Ellie on their phones."

For the first time I realize I'm the only one Dad *hasn't* called since we left home. There's a good chance he won't be allowed to call us after today, either. Guess I won't be hearing from him anytime soon. And that would be all right.

I think.

"Is Dad going to jail?" I ask.

Ron shrugs. "It's possible he won't, with his clean record. But he's likely to get a big fine and that might stop his stalking and phone contacts."

Mom and Marsha look at each other. Say nothing. We all know a fine will just make Dad madder. I've heard the women at the shelter talk. They say most of these guys don't care about laws or restraining orders. They just want to get their way.

Ron's a good lawyer, but did he ever live with someone like Dad? Did he ever sit in a shelter and hear the stories, see the fear?

Ron stands up. "I know these guys are unpredictable, but all we can do is present your case and hope the judge slaps him a good one. Like some time in jail besides the fine. And if Roberto's convicted of the crimes he's committed, we're asking for a Permanent Standing Restraining Order."

"That would be good," Mom says. "Especially if he doesn't go to jail."

"Yes," Ron agrees.

"What about custody?" Ellie asks. "I don't want to live with him."

"Your mom will have to go back to civil court to get custody of you kids, no visitation, and child support. This judge can't deal with those issues, but if she gets her permanent order, there shouldn't be any trouble getting custody, et cetera."

We follow Marsha and him back to the courtroom. It isn't as big as I expected, or as crowded. But it looks pretty much like TV courtrooms. Lots of wood on the walls and lots of wooden furniture. Cool, professional, legal.

No emotions allowed.

We sit on a bench in back, listen to the judge deliver his verdict on another case.

His face is lined, his voice stern. His black robe makes him look enormous.

He's scary, too!

Then Dad and his lawyer walk in. Pass us without a glance. They sit close together half way up and don't talk.

Dad looks confident. I wonder if he knows something we don't.

The air gets thin all of a sudden. I can't breathe, feel sick. If I get called to testify, I'll throw up for sure.

"Tranquility improves performance."

I remember Master Han's lesson on meditation and close my eyes. Repeat "peace" in my head over and over. Breathe deeply. Relax my muscles one at a time. Wish Master Han was here.

"We're up now," Ron says. "Marsha, you and the kids sit behind our table up front, okay?"

He and Mom sit down. Marsha sits between Ellie and me. Pulls out a small pad.

I look over at Dad. He's wearing a new suit, has a fresh haircut. His lawyer has thick white hair and smiles like this is a walk in the park.

Not good. If we have such a great case, why does he look so calm?

Mom takes the stand first. Before she and Ron walk to the judge's bench, we hear Ron say, "I hope there won't be a lot of interruptions, Mercedes, because I'm just going to ask you to tell me what it's been like, living with Roberto."

She nods, but looks pale. Takes a big breath. When she takes the oath, her hand shakes. After she sits down, Ron smiles at her. She smiles back and that seems to help.

"Mrs. Castillo," Ron says, "Could you please point to your husband?"

"He is right there," Mom says, pointing at the other table in front. Her accent is strong and her eyes flicker away from Dad almost immediately.

"Thank you. Now can you describe what marriage to him has been like?"

Mom takes a big breath and talks directly to Ron. "When we got married almost twenty years ago, he already liked things done his way. Before the children came, I had more time so I could follow his instructions. I was young. I thought it was my job to make him happy.

"Once the children came, sixteen and fifteen years ago, his instructions became commands and sometimes I was too busy to do what he wanted. He'd get furious if I didn't respond immediately, even if I was in the middle of feeding or changing the baby."

Dad's lawyer objected but the judge blew it off.

Mom must have thought about her testimony a lot before today. Maybe she even practiced telling her story with Marsha. I don't know. It's just that she told it so convincingly, anyone could see she was telling the truth.

She didn't leave much out, either. Described how she changed over the years from a happy, confident girl to a frightened person with no rights.

Sometimes she had to stop talking because she began to cry. She'd wipe her eyes, look at us and pull herself together. She was like a prisoner of war who had somehow escaped and was determined to tell the world exactly what the enemy did to her.

You could tell from what she said that Dad's control was so harsh there were many times she didn't know what to do. When he threatened to hurt us or Moochie, she'd give in. When he hit her, she couldn't leave because she had two kids and no money. When he was nice again, she thought he'd changed. Being his wife interfered with being our mother and vice versa.

No matter how many times Dad's lawyer objected, the judge always said her testimony was relevant.

By the time she got to why we had to leave Dad and how the shelter helped her, she was sitting up straighter, talking louder. Looking directly at Dad.

I couldn't have done what she did. To me, she was Wonder Woman.

I looked at Dad. His face was serious but not angry. He always was a good actor. He could be screaming at Mom one minute and politely greeting a couple of Girl Scouts selling cookies the next.

Today, he'd put on a mask to hide his fury, but we knew it was there. And we knew what would happen if he had a chance to get Mom back.

"It isn't easy to live in a battered women's shelter," she said. "But it is wonderful to feel safer than I did at home, to see my children feeling safer and living without violence. I don't need Roberto or his abuse anymore. I won't take it. I'm going to make it *without* him."

She raised her chin. "And my children will too."

It's Dad's lawyer who gets to question Mom now, and he isn't smiling.

"Mrs. Castillo, you say this alleged abuse went on for years, but you didn't leave Robert. Why is that?"

Mom took a deep breath. "He wouldn't let me work when the children were small. He gave me only enough money for food and household expenses. I couldn't save much of anything, and I was too proud to go into a shelter."

"He told me I was stupid and no good so many times I began to wonder if he was right. I got so depressed I could hardly take care of the children, but he wouldn't let me go to a psychiatrist."

Dad's lawyer leaned forward, but not in a friendly way. "Didn't you have health insurance so you could visit a doctor on your own, and someone you could leave the children with?"

Mom closed her eyes, took a deep breath.

I hated Dad's lawyer, and hated Dad for hiring him. He wanted the judge to think she had choices, but she didn't.

"Yes, I had insurance," Mom said, "but no money for the co-pay and no one to watch the children. Roberto made me tell my family I was sick or the kids had an event almost every time they invited us over. It got so I only saw them once or twice a year, and if they called me when he was there, he stood over me trying to get me to hang up."

"I was embarrassed at what had happened to me and scared to tell them the truth. It ruined our relationship. They thought I didn't care about them anymore."

"So you say it's Robert's fault you were separated from your family. But tell me, you had a car. Why didn't you visit them when Robert was at work? Why didn't you leave him and live with your parents?"

Mom wiped her eyes. "I was ashamed of my weakness, ashamed that I couldn't do anything right, according to Robert. I always felt tired and sad. I had no energy to get away, even if my parents had had a bigger house and room for me and the kids. But they didn't.

My grandmother already lived with them. My mother couldn't take care of us, too."

"Now I am trying to mend all the damage my lies and excuses did to my relationship with my family. It's very hard."

Dad's lawyer questioned her for what seemed like forever. Mom did her best, but Dad's lawyer hammered her over and over for not doing *something*. He tried to make it seem like she didn't want to leave Dad.

That his treatment couldn't have been that bad or she would have left.

Ellie and I were furious, and Marcia knew it. "The defendant's lawyer always does this," she whispered. "He's trying to destroy her credibility, but he's not doing it because she's hanging tough."

Finally, Mom was allowed to step down.

Ron gave the judge the pictures of the injuries to Moochie, Ellie and Mom that last day at home.

The judge looked them over, dropped them on the desk. Didn't hide his disgust or anger. Next, he read the papers Ellie and I signed. Said we didn't have to testify.

That was a relief, but my insides kept doing somersaults. This day was so important. It could change our whole lives. I never thought I'd say this, but Ellie was right when I complained about living at the shelter. Our life is better without Dad. I hope it stays that way.

"So far, so good," Marsha whispers.

Now it's Dad's turn to testify. First his lawyer interviews him. Tries to makes Mom look like she's hysterical, incompetent, and overreacting. Tries to show that Dad is really the victim.

The judge listens, scowling the whole time. Guess he didn't like the picture of Mom's purple jaw and noticed that Ellie's statement and my statement fit perfectly with Mom's testimony.

He probably figured out that Dad's testimony about that awful Sunday sounded like fiction. Fiction that wasn't well written. He was the victim, rejected by his whole family for an "accident."

Next, Ron grills Dad about how he sees the marriage. It sure is fun listening to Dad's version of our twisted life. Feels like we're all on trial and we all look stupid one way or another. But Dad comes off as a whiner. It was so hard to live with a wife and kids who messed up constantly. Who never changed, no matter how much he helped us.

Ellie sighs. Mom wipes her eyes. My heart feels like it's squeezed in a vise. Dad sounds like a crazy person to me, but what if the judge doesn't see him like I do?

What if the judge gives Dad a fine and no jail time?

I feel like my skin is shrinking so much, it squeezes my heart and throat. What will Dad do to Ellie and me if he shares custody with Mom? He knows we helped her case. Ellie and I took the pictures after he left. Today we signed a statement about his abuse.

This is bad because Dad's nuts and he doesn't respect the law. Who knows how he'll hurt us? Maybe he'll take us far away so Mom has no control. He could hide us in his new basement, tie us up, not let us go to school. Change his name, do day work. Pay cash so no one could find him.

My imagination is out of control again. Gotta stop thinking this way!

I take a deep breath and hope the judge will do something drastic enough to remove Dad from our lives.

Suddenly I heard Rhoda's name being called as a witness. I didn't know she was going to testify, but I'm glad she is. She sees Mom every day at work.

Ron asks her if Mom has changed since she moved into the shelter.

"Oh yes, a lot," Rhoda says. "She jumps every time her office phone rings. She calls the kids' camp every morning to make sure they got there all right. And ever since the day Roberto harassed her at work, she stands at the door and looks all around the parking lot before she approaches her car. I don't think she's eating right either, because she's lost weight."

"Last week, I asked her why she's always tired. She said it's because she wakes up shaking most nights and can't get back to sleep."

The judge listens carefully, writes down a couple things she says.

Marsha testifies next and says pretty much the same things Rhoda said.

After she sits down, the Judge calls Dad back to the witness stand. Takes off his glasses and stares at Dad for a couple minutes.

Dad drops his head, becomes very interested in his hands.

Finally the judge asks, "What injuries did you sustain in all this, Mr. Castillo?"

Dad drags up his "tough childhood," how learning to do everything exactly right made him stronger. Then he complains about his long commute, his fear of getting laid off, and the constant mistakes us kids make. He dumps on Mom's cooking and housekeeping, says she doesn't care about his "needs" and is constantly "disobeying" his rules.

Dad's lawyer looks mad.

There goes their case, I hope. Which was lame to begin with.

When Dad finishes talking, Ron says, "No further questions, Your Honor."

The judge nods. "Thank you, Mr. Castillo." He looks at Dad's lawyer, "Do you want to redirect?"

Dad's lawyer shakes his head.

The judge whacks his gavel. "Court will recess until two o'clock."

Mom and Ron talk a couple minutes. I look everywhere but at Dad and it's killing me. I need to see if he looks different than when he strutted in here today. Or if he's putting on an act like everything's fine.

When the judge leaves the room, Ron stands up and smiles. "You did a great job, Mercedes, and so did your witnesses. After lunch, let's meet outside the courtroom at 1:45, okay?"

Mom nods. Ron shoves his laptop in his briefcase, looks at Dad and quietly reminds us, "Don't forget, he still has a restraining order. Don't talk to him. Call 911 if he follows you or tries to contact you in any way."

Mom turns pale, nods again.

Marsha says, "Looks like he's not leaving anytime soon. Let's walk out together."

We follow her and Ron. I keep my eyes front, wonder if Dad is watching our backs.

It's weird, but I don't feel that scared of him right now. He's a liar and a loser and I'm sick of him still trying to pull the strings. Trying to keep us in line.

But his case isn't going well. He's lost control of us, and I know that kills him. I have to see what he looks like. I turn around and take a quick peek before I step into the hall.

Dad's lawyer is gone and he's sitting face front, ramrod straight. His hands are rolled into fists and his jaw is twitching away.

Looks like Dictator Mode all over again, but he can't do a thing to us right now.

Unless he wins.

If he does, we're almost back to square one. Mom won't be living with him, but she will still be under his thumb. And he'll harass her every way he can.

I don't want to think about it. I want him out of our lives.

And I want him left with no way to push himself back in.

28

FLORIE: *THANKS FOR sending me yor new number.*

Ellie: *girl. u were first on my list.*

Florie: *now give :) what happened at court?*

Ellie: *mom got what she wanted and dad got what he deserved.*

Florie: *tell me.*

Ellie: *the criminal court judge gave him a huge fine and gave mom a permanent standing restraining order. that puts dad out of the picture.*

Florie: *wow. so r u all set.*

Ellie: *yeah now we r but we had to go back to civil court so mom could get custody till we r 18. she got that and no visitation and she got child support. dad has to send it to our lawyer's office. that way he wont know our address.*

Florie: *i hope u kissed the judge. oops. judges.*

Ellie: *probly should have. they seemed to be on our side which made dad so mad he got nasty. especially in criminal court. almost got contempt of court.*

Florie: *what was he thinking?*

Ellie: *when he s mad he doesnt think. his lawyer told him 2 shut up 3 times. he finally did. then he looked sad. i dont care if he s sad. its 2 late.*

Florie: *at least u can move back home now.*

Ellie: *no way. mom doesnt trust him. will probly get a divorce when she can deal. right now she s too busy looking for a new job. getting a post office box. sending us 2 a new high school.*

Florie:

Ellie: *what?*

Florie: *sounds like i will never see u again.*

Ellie: *r u crazy. u r sleepin over soon as we get r apartment.*

Florie: *whew. uh oh. poppi is steamin. prob saw my fone bill.*

Ellie: *at least he gets mad 4 a reason.*

Florie: *yeah. gotta go.*

Ellie: *luv u.*

Florie: *luv u back.*

ELLIE: *WHAT UP. can u talk now?*

Florie: *yeah. poppi did his lecture thing but turns out he wasnt pissed about my fone bill.*

Ellie: *so what was wrong?*

Florie: *he found my credit card bill. which is worse. said no mall 4 a month.*

Ellie: *great. whose gonna come shopping with me? help me buy cool school stuff?*

Florie: *me of course. dad will cave. give him a couple days.*

Ellie: *wish my dad was like that. he never caves. cant believe i still miss him sometimes. i must b nuts.*

Florie: *nah. he s your father. course u miss him.*

Ellie: *dont know why. he s a rat. i m so anti men right now. like theres this boy at work. adrian. seems nice but i cant trust him.*

Florie: *why not.*

Ellie: *cuz he s 2 nice. like today. he fixed my register when it jammed. later he made me a big latte and offered me a ride home. i gave him an excuse and he actually accepted it.*

Florie: *woo hoo. girl. better give him a chance.*

Ellie: *i dunno. dee was nice at first 2. though he probly wouldnt offer 2 change his hours in case i have trouble with my register again.*

Florie: *wow.*

Ellie: *yeah. but it might b all 4 show. btw thanks for the sleepover. i loved staying out late n sleeping in. thank your mom for the spanish food. it meant a lot to me.*

Florie: *no big deal. she misses u bad.*

Ellie: *same here. maybe she can visit a while when u sleep over.*

Florie: *sure. oops. poppi s headed my way again. probly found my fone bill.*

Ellie: *u are out of control.*

Florie: *4 sure. hey. dont forget. give adrian a chance.*

Ellie: *maybe. see ya soon.*

DIEGO: *HOW DID court go?*

Dad: *terrible. cant see my kids till they re 18 but still have to pay child support.*

Diego: *that aint fair.*

Dad: *the worst thing is mercedes plans to divorce me.*

Diego: *why? u didnt put them in the hospital or nothing.*

Dad: *no kidding. my problem is when i get something in my mind it won't go away. mercedes is my wife. i love her. i gotta get her back.*

Diego: *same with me and ellie. i still look 4 her evry day.*

Dad: *better you than me. she s on my restraining order too. hey. do you know where my wife works?*

Diego: *sure but she wont have nothin 2 do with me. wont even let ellie date me cuz of the fite and everything.*

Dad: *maybe not but she cant stop you from talking to ellie if you happen to see her in public.*

Diego: *right. or at mcdonalds. :) and she wont know if i follow ellie back to the shelter either.*

Dad: *exactly. so any time you want to borrow the truck its yours. we have to find them before they move.*

Diego: *i m on it.*

29

I GAVE CARTER his second Tae Kwon Do lesson after camp today. Taught him more than moves. Taught him like Master Han taught me. Self-control, respect for everyone. Kindness. He needs to figure out men don't have to be mean and tough.

"I thought Tae Kwon Do was about power," he said after a few minutes.

"That's what I thought at first, too. But it's really about perfecting your moves," I tell him. "It's not about hurting people. The only time you can use the moves is in true self-defense."

Carter frowns. "Too bad my stupid stepfather isn't around. I'd kick him a good one."

"Would that be self-defense?"

He scuffs the ground with his toe. "Yeah. He beat on me, too."

I had to think for a minute. Carter didn't need a lecture on how bad these guys are. He already knew.

"Dad didn't hit me," I said. "He beat me with words. Constant criticism, always expecting perfection, always pushing me to do more than I could. But every time he hit Mom, I wished he was hitting me instead."

Carter wiped his eyes, said, "Me, too," so soft I almost missed it.

"But remember, you can't use Tae Kwon Do for revenge, no matter what! 'Do' stands for a life of self-control and being good to others. Tae can be used only for self-defense. For mortal danger to you."

"Okay, okay." He was crying harder now, wiping his eyes on his shirt.

Then he straightened up. Rolled his hands into fists like he was ready to fight. "Whatcha lookin' at, boy?"

"Hey, I'm not your stepdad. I'm not going to make fun of you or tell anyone what you say or do."

He wipes his nose and looks at me different. "For real?"

"For real."

We go inside, more like friends now. Which is kind of unbelievable.

I'll keep trying with him. I think he's beginning to get it.

We head for our rooms, don't speak, don't have to sneak. Someone decided this week that kids twelve and up can spend time in their own rooms without an adult. Sure beats needing "babysitters" or having to stay downstairs watching bad movies.

In the room, Ellie's perched on the edge of her bed. She's throwing pillows, shirts, shoes—you name it—at *my* bunk.

"Hey!" I yell. "Cut it out! Mess up your own space, okay?"

"What space? I don't have two beds like you! Girls need more than two dresser drawers for everything! I'm tired of this!"

I could remind her how happy she was to move to the shelter, but that wouldn't do any good. Especially since I don't want to go home, either.

I push her stuff aside and sit down next to her. "What's wrong?"

She tosses her phone to me. "Check out my calls."

It takes a while. "Hey, there's only thirty or forty from Dee. Is that the problem? You don't have time to answer all of them?"

"No, stupid! I want to know how he got my new number. I only gave it to Florie."

"Only gave it to Florie? Think about it. She probably gave it to another friend of yours. Then they gave it to someone else and on and on. Until Dee got it."

She punches her pillow. "Damn! I hate him." She wipes her eyes. "And I miss him."

"You said the same thing the last time you guys broke up. You sound like Uncle Humberto."

Mom's brother is one serious alcoholic. Lost everything a few years ago. Finally stopped drinking, got his wife and kids back. Found a good job. Says he still wants to drink every single day.

I sit on Ellie's bed. She's tearing a wad of tissues into little pieces. "Anything else bugging you?"

She looks away.

"Come on, talk."

She sighs. "Okay. I think this truck is following me."

I jump up. "Dad's?"

"No, it's small and white."

"Where'd you see it?"

"First time? Outside McDonald's, twice in one day! The next night, I'm walking home from work and it rolls up behind me, going slow. I tried to see the driver, but he kept looking away."

"So what did you do?"

"What do you think I did? That was the third time I saw the truck in two days! I was so mad I turned around and headed straight for him."

"Are you nuts? He could be psycho! Or a pervert with a weapon!"

"I know, so I pulled out my Mace. I had to know who was buggin' me!"

She's got mace?

"You should have called 911."

Her eyebrows shoot up. Neck gets snaky. "Right, like they would have caught him. The *second* he saw me coming, he did a U-ie and took off!"

"Guess he wasn't some guy checking you out."

She starts pacing. "No, those guys say 'Hey,' act friendly. You know."

"Not really. No guys have checked me out lately."

She rolls her eyes. "Look, all I know is this guy made sure I didn't see him. I figured I spooked him and he was gone for good. But after camp yesterday, there he is again!"

"Why didn't you tell me?"

"I wasn't working last night so I didn't bother. But this afternoon he parked at the dry cleaners *next* to the mart."

"Maybe he was dropping off clothes."

"Don't think so. Remember how we got off the bus today and I went in the mart to buy gum and you headed back here?"

"Yeah. Damn. You should have told me. If I knew he was there, I'd have gone after him."

"Well I didn't know he was there, either. Didn't see him 'til I came outside again and then I was so shocked I just stood there and stared."

"Did you get his plate number?"

"No."

"Could you see who it was?"

"No! He was wearing that big cap again. I pulled out my Mace and moved his way. Naturally, he took off."

"He keeps hiding his face, so he's gotta be someone you know."

"Hey, that's right! Guess you've learned something, reading all those detective novels."

I start pacing, though there wasn't much room for that. "It can't be Dad, not after he got that big fine. What about Diego? He'd love to follow you here."

I sat down and it hit me like a slap. "Oh my God! I saw a small white truck on the road at the park, that Sunday Diego bugged us! Maybe he did borrow the truck and now he's stalking you with it!"

Ellie thinks a minute, nods slowly. "Diego. Yeah, he could definitely be the one stalking me, he's so desperate to know where I live." She thumps her head. "Why didn't I listen to Ron and get a restraining order on Dee?"

Her phone rings. She checks the number, shakes her head. "I can't believe it. It's him."

"Gimme the phone. I'll get rid of his ass. He needs to leave you alone."

She slumps down on her bed. "No, what if Mom comes in while you're talking to him? She'll figure out what's going on and I'll be in deep shit. I'll text him later, tell him to stop contacting me or I'll call the police."

"Why? He won't admit what he's doing because he's like Dad. Anything he does is okay because he's never wrong. And he's stubborn. He'll probably try to follow you again."

Like tonight . . .OMG! She's working tonight!

"What time you get off work?"

"Ten."

"Okay. I'll meet you, walk you home."

"Thanks, but did you forget about curfew?"

"Shit."

I think a minute. "Look, this is getting bad. We've gotta tell Mom what's going on. What if the driver isn't Dee? Could be someone worse. We don't know! Please, let Mom pick you up tonight!"

"Forget it! If you tell her I'm being stalked, she'll make me quit my job and she'll call the police! Listen, I promise I'll speed dial 911 if I see the truck again."

"Promise?"

"Yes! Now shut up, *Dad.*"

My stomach growls. "Yeah, yeah. Come on, let's go eat. I think Bev's making tacos."

I'm right. A big plate on the breakfast bar is stacked high with beef and bean tacos. We take three each. Slap on lettuce, tomato bits, cheese, and salsa.

We can always count on Bev and Keesh to cook what we like.

"Thanks for making tacos, Bev," I say when we sit down at Mom's table. I'm trying to let the women know I'm not always a jerk.

"You're welcome," she smiles and crunches into one.

Carter shows up. Fills a plate and sits down next to me. Mom's talking with Keesh and Bev at the table. She's smiling, looks excited. Is eating like she enjoys food again.

"Hey, I found a good apartment today," she says when we sit down. "And I put a deposit on it."

"Tell us!" Ellie says.

"It's the first floor of a two-family house. The neighborhood is clean and the houses are kept up real well."

"What about bedrooms?" I ask.

Mom laughed. "I knew you'd both want your own room. And it has three bedrooms!"

Now Ellie and I are practically bouncing on our chairs.

"How about laundry?" Ellie asks.

"No problem. There's a washer and dryer in the cellar, and the kitchen's big. There's even a hoop in the back yard! The owners live upstairs and have a baby boy. They seem friendly."

"Sounds real good," I say. "Does it have a garage?"

Mom sighs. "No. I'll have to park on the street."

"How many bathrooms?" Ellie asks.

"Only one," Mom says. "But it's a split bath with two sinks so it'll be easier for us to get ready in the morning."

"What about Moochie? Can we take Moochie?"

Mom laughs. "That's the first thing I asked. And the answer is...YES!"

She has energy, happiness. Looks so good we're all smiling.

Ellie and I yell "Yaaaaay!" at the same time.

I feel like I could fly. We're getting Moochie back *and* we'll each have our own room!

"When do we move?" I ask. "I'll pack, carry boxes. Whatever."

"I'm shooting for Saturday," Mom says, smiling. "Brenda's brother promised to let us use his truck, and he's driving!"

"Wow, that's great." I remember him from Brenda's last bar-b-que. He's big and strong. Which we might need if Dad's home and acts like a jerk. He's not supposed to come anywhere near us, but he will. Rules are for the other guy, not him.

My heart speeds up. I've wanted to move out of the shelter since we got here, and the apartment sounds perfect for us. But going back home first is scary. Dad will try to monitor our every move, that's for sure.

The other thing that's making me nervous is all the changes. In three days, we'll be in a new home and new neighborhood. Then two days later, a new school! That's at least two too many changes for me.

Carter says, "So you're moving out of the shelter, Mike?"

Uh, oh. I forgot he was at our table. His forehead's crinkled and he isn't eating.

"Yeah, but we're on a bus line. You can visit and we'll practice Tae together, okay?"

He nods but doesn't smile. "Mom's looking for a place, too but I don't know if it'll be in the city."

"Let's hope it is," I say. "And one more thing. Could you call me Miguel from now on? I'll have a new home. Need a new name."

Mom laughs like I gave her a million bucks, and Ellie smiles big. Carter looks confused.

"Mike is my dad's name for me," I explain. "But he won't be around and Mom and Ellie always call me Miguel."

He nods. "Oh, okay. Sure." He turns away, stares out the window.

Too bad we're leaving right when Carter and I are becoming friends. When he's beginning to think a little straighter.

But I'm not sorry to go. An apartment's way better than living in one room. Plus, it seems like shelter women keep their friends. Mom will probably come back for group, and I bet Keesh and Bev will visit us at the apartment.

Mom borrows a pencil. Starts making a list. "I can't believe how much I have do this week, and how much stuff we have to retrieve from the house."

Ellie starts tapping on the table. "But Dad's still living there. What about that permanent restraining order? Doesn't he have to leave when we show up?"

Mom makes a face. "No, it's his house, too. He can stay on the property, but the order says he has to keep his distance. He'd better, or I'll call 911."

The way she says it, the anger in her eyes, the tightness of her mouth—I believe she wants to do that. But I wonder what will happen if he gets real nasty. She'll want to make peace so we can get out of there.

She checks her list. Scribbles some more.

"What about school?" I ask.

She sighs, then smiles again. "We lucked out there. Central High is only two blocks from the apartment, so you can walk every day—together."

"Great!" Ellie says. "Miguel can protect me from all the big, bad boys."

"Yeah. Like you'd let me."

Mom shakes her head. "This is crazy. We have three days to move and set up the apartment. Then two days after that, you kids start school!"

My mood tanks. A new school.

"I wish we could go to our old one," I say. "City schools are big and we won't know anybody."

"Right, but don't forget the good part—Dad won't know where we are," Ellie says.

I nod. "Word." There's a lot to be said for not having to constantly watch the streets for him.

Mom smiles. "At least you'll both be in the same school. I admit some of the kids might be tougher than what you're used to, but you've run into bullies before."

"You mean like Dad?" Ellie asks.

Mom shrugs. "If the shoe fits . . . And speaking of shoes, we've gotta hit the mall tomorrow. You need sneakers, jeans, and a couple shirts, Miguel. How about you, working girl?"

Ellie smiles. "I'm okay except for a new book bag."

I can't believe how cool she looks. You'd never know she's afraid Dee will be stalking her again tonight. She pulls out her phone, checks the time. "Yikes! Gotta go to work!"

The butterflies in my stomach do their thing, and I can't finish my last taco.

Somehow I have to walk Ellie home from work tonight. Watch for a truck that's probably driven by a nut. And not get caught lying to Mom or breaking curfew.

What I'd really like to do is climb up on my bunk and go to sleep.

But I'm a good guy.

I'll figure it out. And I'll do it, for my sister.

30

BRENDA: *HEY IS it okay if my brother brings along his weight lifting buddy to help u move?*

Mom: *its more than ok. roberto wont try anything with two strong men behind me.*

Brenda: *unless he goes ballistic. maybe we should bring the police with us.*

Mom: *i m hoping we can do it this way. other women at the shelter have. don't worry. if he gets rotten i will call 911.*

Brenda: *u sure its safe?*

Mom: *safer than bringing the police with us which would upset the kids and neighbors and probly set him off.*

Brenda: *ok. tough call but you gotta go with yor gut.*

Mom: *thanks 4 understanding. btw i m filling up the new fridge tonight. tell the guys i m doing lunch for the crew on saturday.*

Brenda: *sounds good. when u want us to show up?*

Mom: *hows nine a.m. saturday at the house?*

Brenda: *good. we will meet you there.*

Mom: *thanks. yor the best.*

◞   ◞   ◞

DIEGO: *PROBLEM MR. c. ellie made the truck yesterday but not me. i got away. mayb i parked 2 close 2 the mart.*

Dad: *next time park a couple blocks away and walk back. watch from across the street.*

Diego: *ok. i dont work tonite so i can case mcdonalds. follow ellie home.*

Dad: *i told u. dont go to her job.*

Diego: *but that was before court. its safe now rite?*

Dad: *not if ellie freaks out and u get arrested 4 stalking.*

Diego: *i aint stalkin. just making a friendly visit.*

Dad: *dont do it. it will scare her. she might call 911 or get fired.*

Diego: *okay. but i cant find your family no other way. just one more try okay?*

Dad: *i dont know. u are getting careless.*

Diego: *i promise i will park the truck down the street and b real careful.*

Dad: *still sounds risky.*

Diego: *u want me to find out where they live or not? i never seen miguel on the street. not once. and i cant follow your wife. she will call 911 if she makes me.*

Dad: *u got that right. ok. i guess theres no other choice. come over at seven.*

Diego: *thanks. ttyl.*

BILLY: *OKAY. GOT yor back. u hafta walk ellie home after curfew so the story is my moms pickin u up at the mart at 9 tonite and yor stayin at my house. then she s droppin u back at the mart tomorrow.*

Miguel: *u got it. thanx.*

Billy: *but really. where r u stayin overnite? the citys dangerous.*

Miguel: *i dunno. maybe i can sleep in the bus station.*

Billy: *yeah that will work. good luck.*

ಌ   ಌ   ಌ

DAD: I M STILL *worried about you going to mcdonalds. if you go to ellies job she might get mad. what if you get mad back and do something stupid. you know how tough she acts when she s mad. she might call 911 and that makes me nervous. call or text me soon as you see this. thanks.*

Diego:

31

I'VE NEVER LIED this bad to Mom, but I must be getting better at it. She believed me! She thinks I'm sleeping at Billy's tonight. When she wasn't around, I stuffed a blanket and game in my backpack plus a couple juices and PB&J's.

All set.

I kiss her goodbye. "See ya tomorrow morning."

"Good. Have fun, but don't forget you've still gotta pack for the move. Got your toothbrush?"

Of course not.

I grab it and take off. In the office, I write a note to the woman talking on the Hot Line. "Have a sleepover tonight. I'm leaving now. Mom knows."

She nods, covers the receiver. "Don't forget to sign out."

Arrrrrgh! The apartment is looking better and better.

Only a sliver of the moon in the sky but no prob. Plenty of streetlights and traffic to show the way. I take my time. Reach MacDonald's by 9:00. Gives me an hour to make sure no one shows up in a white truck.

I walk around to the back. Check out every vehicle in the drive thru line and parking lot.

No trucks in any color.

Return to the front of the building, look through the front door. Ellie's not working the counter. Must be doing Pick Up.

I circle the building so I can check out the Pick Up side. Yup. It's her voice squawking through the order box. "That'll be seven eighty-five. Second window, please."

I cross the parking lot and squeeze behind tall bushes opposite the pickup window. Ellie's real busy taking orders, packing them, making change. I glance back at the line of cars.

Almost freak. See a small white truck stop and order something at the box!

I can't see the driver's face, but I'm pretty sure it's a man.

I'm juiced. Maybe this is the stalker! I can hardly wait for the two cars in front of him to pick up their orders. I pull out pencil and paper. Prepare to write down the plate number. Meanwhile, I smell burgers, fries, and fish, but I'm too scared to feel hungry. All I feel is kind of sick.

When the truck pulls up to the window, I can't hear a word. Ellie frowns, shakes her head. Doesn't take money from the driver or hand him food. Jumps when he shouts something. Shuts the window and signals for the manager.

I try to read his plate, but I'm facing the side of the truck, not the back. Better call 911. Reach in my pocket for my new phone.

Not there!

Then I remember. It's in my backpack. No time to look for it. I have to get the plate number. I push through the bushes, step onto the blacktop. This is my last chance.

The truck squeals away. Didn't get the number. I'm shaking too hard to write it down anyway.

An older man steps into the booth, listens to Ellie. Nods.

I hope she knows who was driving that truck.

32

MOM: *SORRY 2 call so late but i m a wreck.*

    Brenda: *whats wrong?*

    Mom: *ellie s working tonite. she should be back by now but hasnt called and isnt answering her cell.*

    Brenda: *thats not like her. does she have a new boyfriend?*

    Mom: *she mentioned someone at work but nothing serious far as i know. i hope diego didnt talk her into going 4 a ride.*

    Brenda: *me too. have u called her friends?*

    Mom: *i called florie but she s working 2. mcdonalds fone has been busy so i m driving there now. its after curfew but i got permission.*

    Brenda: *maybe the shelter will let miguel help u look 4 her.*

    Mom: *he cant. he s at billys house tonite.*

    Brenda: *call me when u find her okay?*

    Mom: *i will. thanks girlfriend.*

33

ELLIE'S STILL TALKING to the manager and a new guy's working the window.

I am about to pee my pants and breathing like I got a bag over my head. What if the truck comes back?

I need the Cavalry, the Marines. Someone to help me before I chicken out. Run and hide.

I wait 'til the last car in line picks up its order and leaves. Then I grab my backpack and run to the window. Bang on it twice.

The new guy jumps, turns around and yells, "Hey, Frank!"

Ellie and the manager look over.

"Miguel!" Ellie squeaks.

I was afraid she'd be mad, but she looks relieved to see me!

"That's my brother, Frank. He can walk me home."

"Oh, good." The manager sticks his head out. Points to a door twenty feet away from the window. "Wait down there. She'll be out in a couple minutes."

I do what he says, but I'm scared shitless standing out in the open. I watch for Psycho to return. Pace back and forth. Hope the door isn't locked if the truck shows up again.

Finally, it opens a crack. Ellie whispers, "You there, Miguel?"

"Yeah."

"Is it safe?"

I check the street and the short line of cars approaching toward the pickup window. "Yeah. Let's go."

She steps outside, grabs my hand. Hers is shaky and damp. I wish Mom was here with us. Finally, Ellie's showing she's scared. She'd tell Mom everything.

"I don't know how ya did it, Miguel," she says, "but I'm glad you're here. Thanks."

Her voice is shaky, too, which makes me even more scared. I hope she can hold it together until we get back to the shelter.

"Is Dee gone?" she asks, looking at the street.

"You mean . . . so Dee was driving the truck?"

She nods. "Yeah. We guessed right. He must have borrowed it so he could stalk me!"

"Well, at least we know. Now we can tell Mom and the police."

She pulls her hand away. "The police? Do we have to?"

What is this? She still wants to protect the Psycho?

This is no time to fight about Dee. "Never mind. Let's just get outta here before he comes back."

Her eyes pop and we take off. We stop at the sidewalk, look up and down the street. It's pretty dark even with all the commercial lights, but you can tell what's a truck and what's a car.

"I don't see him," I say. My insides are jelly, but somehow my voice comes out steady.

We jog a couple blocks before she asks, "How did you ever con Mom into letting you stay out this late?"

The adrenaline in my blood turns to sludge. With all this excitement, I forgot what I did to get here. I am in soooo much trouble. "I'll tell ya later. Let's just get back to the shelter, okay?"

She shrugs. "Okay."

We reach our corner. Cross the street without waiting for the signal. No sign of the truck.

I breathe easier. "Two more blocks and we're home free, Ell!"

She smiles. "Thanks to you, bro."

Oops. I forgot. She's home free, not me!

"Um . . . just one problem. You have to sneak me in, okay?"

She stops dead. Plants her fists on her waist. Eyes flash, neck gets snaky. "I should've known! You're breaking curfew, right? And lemme guess. Mom doesn't know you're out here."

"Yeah. I lied, like somebody else I know."

"So? I'm older than you, don't forget!"

She is furious, nasty, tough as nails.

I smile. Just like the old days.

"Keep your shorts on, Ell. I didn't want you walking home alone, okay? I told Mom I was going to Billy's for a sleepover."

Her eyebrows lift. "Oh, that's why you have a backpack."

"Yeah."

"My hero!" she yells and hugs me.

Whoa, this is a first. And a mistake. We aren't paying attention to traffic.

Just like that, a small white truck screeches to a stop at the curb, not four feet from us.

We're too shocked to move, but Diego isn't. He hops out, runs over to us, and shoves me so hard I fall on my butt. Before I can get up, he grabs Ellie's arm. Tries to drag her to the truck.

"Let go, asshole!" she yells. Yanks her arm away.

He grabs her again. Pushes her against a tree. Crosses her arms at the wrist and pins her with his chest.

She's screaming, trying to kick him.

"Cut it!" he yells. "And listen to me, bitch. You are *my girl and nobody else's.* I seen you gettin' friendly with that guy at work. You better get unfriendly fast, or he's gonna have a couple broken legs. You got that?"

Whoa. He is as bad as Dad! I get up, stand behind them. Whip my phone out and dial 911.

Ellie screams again. Diego covers her mouth.

I shout into the phone. Want the dispatcher to hear me. Want Asshole to hear me.

"This is Miguel Castillo. I'm on Polanzie Street near the corner. My sister's ex-boyfriend is trying to kidnap her. We need help. Hurry, please!"

"Don't hang up!" the woman says. "Look around. Tell me the closest address."

I give her the number on the building behind us. Hang up, throw myself at Dee's back. He swings around, lets go of Ellie. She falls on the ground. He punches me in the gut so hard I crumple.

A car screeches to a stop near us. I look at it, pray it's not one of Diego's friends. Force myself to sit up. Dee isn't moving, seems paralyzed by the headlights!

Ellie stands up and yells, "It's Adrian! Adrian! Help us!"

Adrian—the guy from work.

He hops out of the car. Is tall and super skinny. I hope he's stronger than he looks.

Diego checks him out, sneers, "You got a problem?"

Great. Psycho's back.

Dee whirls around, grabs Ellie. Throws her over his shoulder fireman style. Her feet dangle down his front, her upper body is bent over his shoulder.

He heads for the truck. Ellie tries to push herself off him. Grunts, digs her nails into his back, screams, "Help, somebody help!"

Cars slow down and gawk, but no one stops. Adrian's standing behind Dee's car. He's on the phone. Giving 911 the plate number, I hope.

I beat Diego to the truck. Check the passenger door. It's locked. Good, he can't throw her in on that side.

My butt hurts bad but I run around to the driver's side and look in. Yes! He left his keys in the ignition. I grab them, shove them in my pocket. Lock that door, too.

By the time I get back to the curb, my upside down sister has her teeth locked on Diego's back.

"Bitch!" he screams and tries to pull her body around to the front. She keeps biting and grabs his belt in back so he can't pull her off him.

Adrian runs behind Dee and jump-kicks the back of his knees. Hard.

The creep falls forward with Ellie still hanging on.

"Let go, Ellie!" I yell.

She drops to the ground, rolls away from him.

Dee is face down on the sidewalk, moaning.

I run over and sit on his butt. Hold his arms down with my feet. Adrian pins his legs and Ellie leans on his head, says, "You ain't goin' nowhere, ass wipe."

Dee swears, begs, tries to twist sideways. Almost gets one arm free.

I press down harder. Smell diesel, Indian food, victory.

Dee turns his head sideways. "Get off me or you're dead. I got friends."

"Yeah? Where are they now?" I ask. "In jail, like you're gonna be?"

The wail of a police siren fills the street.

Dee drops his forehead to the sidewalk. "Okay, okay. I give," he says. "Just let me up."

"Sure thing," I say. Don't move. No one else does, either.

The police car blocks Dee's truck and an officer jumps out. "What's going on here?"

While we're telling him, he cuffs Diego and I see Mom's car. If I weren't so pumped, I think I'd die.

She pulls past us real slow. Parks a couple spaces up. Must have come looking for Ellie, saw us on the sidewalk.

Which will be hard to explain since I'm supposed to be at Billy's house.

I am so dead.

Then I remember. Diego's in more trouble than me, and he doesn't stand a chance of explaining this away.

Besides, I did something good. I kept my sister safe. Maybe Mom will understand and not kill me for all the lies.

34

FLORIE: *GIRL. U gotta b so stressed. movin. startin a new school next week.*

Ellie: *i am and i miss u bad. esp. after last nite.*

Florie: *what happened?*

Ellie: *dee hassled me at work. after i left he tried to kidnap me. miguel and adrian stopped him. police arrested his ass.*

Florie: *wow. so he s off yor back.*

Ellie: *not really. he will get out on bail so i still have to get a restraining order against him.*

Florie: *why bother? after u move dee s history.*

Ellie: *except he knows where i go to school now.*

Florie: *huh?*

Ellie: *yeah. he called all the high schools. said he was my uncle manny and mom was in a bad accident. told them he was from out of town and needed my new address. the other schools didnt have my name but the secretary at my new school asked him to hold while she found the vice principal.*

Florie: *how do u know all that?*

Ellie: *the v.p. called me at home later. said he called mom. found out i dont have an uncle manny and that she was fine. said he asked the caller 4 his name and he hung up.*

Florie: *then how did they know it was diego?*

Ellie: *the office has caller i d. and dee used his cell.*

Florie: *wow. smart move.*

Ellie: *yeah but good 4 me cuz the v.p. gave me a statement for court. marsha says i can get a restraining order no sweat.*

Florie: *u rock. keep in touch ok. xo*

Ellie: *for sure. luv u.*

BILLY: *SO HOW did u like our sleepover?*

Miguel: *forget it. i m so busted. mom went looking for ellie when she didn't get back from work on time. caught us on the street with diego and the police.*

Billy: *wow. u grounded for life or what?*

Miguel: *not after mom and the shelter heard what happened.*

Billy: *so tell me.*

Miguel: *dee tried to kidnap ellie on her way home. a guy from mcdonalds drove by an helped us.*

Billy: *lucky he came along.*

Miguel: *wasnt luck. he likes ellie. the manager told him about dee s visit an he went looking 4 us.*

Billy: *sounds like an ok guy.*

Miguel: *yeah. he fought hard. helped us a lot. btw we r moving 2 morrow. i will call u about a sleepover next week.*

Billy: *great. ttyl.*

FLORIE: *HOW WAS court?*

Ellie: *got my restraining order. told adrian i could go to the movies with him after we move.*

Florie: *who hoo!*

Ellie: *yeah. but dont spread rumors about adrian and me. i m goin slow. so far he treats me right. if that changes he s history.*

Florie: *ok. i wont say a word till u and adrian r tight. or not. hows soccer this year?*

Florie: *good except dad showed up at my first game. dee probly told him about my new school.*

Florie: *did yor mom call 911?*

Ellie: *not right away but miguel was at the game. he snuck back to the parking lot when he saw dad. found out the white truck is dads cuz it had all his fishing gear in the back seat. he got the plate number. ran back to the bleachers. recited the number to dad. loud. asked did he forget about the restraining order? dad left fast. then mom called 911.*

Florie: *cant believe wussy miguel got yor dads ass in a sling. now u can go home n get yor stuff. he wont even be there 2 bug u.*

Ellie: *yes he will. he always makes bail. but he s gonna be sooo mad at us. he will probly get another big fine. but get this. we have 2 big guys helping us move thanks to a friend of moms.*

Florie: *girl. thats great. tell miguel he s my hero. i didnt know he was so cool.*

Ellie: *yeah. guess all that detective stuff paid off. btw mom says u can sleep over next week.*

Florie: *yaaaaay! just tell me when. luv u.*

Ellie: *me 2.*

35

THIS IS IT—Saturday, the day we go home and pick up our stuff. Soon as I get there, I'm grabbing everything I own—my clothes, posters, games, *everything!*

But it's scary. Who knows what we'll find at the house? Maybe Dad's changed the furniture around. Filled the fridge with beer and takeout. Trashed our stuff.

What I hate is, it's still his house, too. He can be on the property when we're there. He'll find a way to harass us—I know he will!

And I don't know what I'll do if he tries to order us around or treats Mom bad. I'm not going to jump when he yells. I'm not going to "Yes, Dad" him when he expects stupid things.

That's the plan, anyway.

Maybe I'm getting worked up for nothing. Maybe a miracle will happen, like he'll act decent, disappear for a while. Let us take our stuff and leave.

Right. Like Dad would turn control of *anything* over to *anyone.*

He must have been on my mind this morning, because I woke up in the middle of a bad dream. Bev goes back home with Jenna and Holly to pick up their things. Her husband's there and they have a great reunion—cat and mouse games. Fear, anger, control.

No wonder I woke up scared. It's what I'm afraid will happen to us today.

Okay. Change of plan. I'm not going back to my house. I'm staying in bed under the covers.

Except that won't work. I've gotta pick my old room clean. Otherwise, Dad will destroy whatever's left.

The good news is that Brenda's bringing Moochie with her today. He'll come straight to the apartment with us! But once we actually get there, he's staying in Mom's car so he'll be safe.

I get up, get dressed, eat some cereal.

We head for our house right after breakfast. Mom's gripping the steering wheel so hard her fingers are white. Ellie's "reading" a magazine. (Hasn't turned a page.)

I'm sitting in the back seat praying Dad is out of town. Or at least off the premises.

The small moving truck's already parked at the curb. Brenda's sitting in the cab with her six-foot-two brother Fred and his best friend, Bob.

Bob's big, too. Has muscles on his muscles, three earrings, and a short Mohawk.

Yeah! Two points for our side.

Just one problem. Dad's posed in front of the garage, Dictator style: arms crossed in front, legs spread, jaw muscle twitching. Naturally, he's standing right where the moving truck should go.

When we arrive, Brenda's brother Fred parks the truck straight across the end of the driveway. He can't drive in, but no one can drive out, either.

Mom nods. "I guess he knows how to play the same games as Dad."

We watch Dad and the truck, waiting for trouble. A minute later, Brenda, Fred, and Bob hop out of the truck. They have a plan, I think. Brenda leans against the truck, holding Moochie tight. Fred and Bob head up the driveway.

Me, I'm about to pee my pants because I just remembered Dad's shotgun. Grandpa used it for hunting. Dad said that's why he kept it. Only he never hunted. Just pulled the gun out when Mom gave him what he called a "hard time."

Owning a gun is a no-no if you have a Restraining Order, so it better be gone.

Knowing Dad, it isn't.

Ellie's shaking. Mom pats her knee, says, "Don't worry, honey. Fred helped someone else move out on a guy like Dad. He knows what to do. The restraining order doesn't involve him or Bob, either, so they can talk to Dad. We'll wait here until they take care of this."

The two big guys walk up the driveway. Stop directly in front of Dad. Fold their arms across their chests and stare down at him, since they're about six inches taller.

Dad stares back, says nothing.

I roll down the window. Maybe I can learn something about how to deal with control freaks.

Fred jerks a thumb toward the truck but his eyes stay on Dad. "We need to park closer to the house. You got a problem with that?"

The muscle in Dad's jaw twitches double time. Finally, he looks away. "I guess not, as long as I see everything, and I mean *every. Single. Thing.* That leaves my house before it's loaded on the truck."

Fred and Bob say nothing.

Dad leans back against the garage, arms still crossed in front of him. Throws the guys a nasty, hard stare like he's in charge.

Only he just gave in.

As soon as Fred starts to back the truck up the driveway, Dad disappears around the side of the house.

I hope he'll stay outside and leave us alone.

"The women at the shelter are right," Mom says, pointing in Dad's direction. "Bullies are cowards."

"And jerks," Ellie adds.

We leave our car parked on the street in front of the house. Brenda walks over and gives Moochie to Mom. "He'll be okay in the car with the windows rolled down a little. It's not that hot."

Mom nods, lets us hold him a minute. He looks good, but whines and licks us like crazy.

"Okay, time to get going," Mom says.

I set Moochie on the back seat. "I don't like leaving him alone."

"Me, either," Mom says, "but he'll be safer here."

"I'll stay with him a few minutes," Brenda says and rolls all the car windows down two or three inches.

"Thanks," Mom says. She fills Moochie's water bowl from a bottle and sets it on the floor in the back seat.

Then she unlocks the trunk. We grab as many flattened boxes and leaf bags as we can hold and head for the front door. Wait for Mom. She opens the door, or tries to.

It's locked!

Mom shakes her head, mutters, "The flaming . . . " Pulls out her keys and lets us in. Me, I'd love to leave some handprints on its perfect paint job. Inconvenience the Dictator for a change.

I look into the living room. Where is he, anyway?

We follow Mom into the kitchen. Stand still and listen.

It's too quiet, inside and outside.

"I hope he's still out back," Mom says, "and stays there! Anyway, here's the plan. We pack up our bedrooms while the guys take apart the beds and carry the big stuff out."

I walk back through the living room, cross the foyer, and step through the door into the garage. "Better make sure he didn't lock the outside garage door, too."

Mom nods. "Good idea."

It lifts easily.

Fred and Bob have opened the back of the truck, which is parked about ten feet from the garage. They pull down the ramp, toss out old quilts and more boxes.

I jump when the lawnmower roars into action behind the house.

Fred smiles. "Good. Now we know where your Dad is."

When I get upstairs, I turn the knob on my bedroom door.

It's locked, too!

"Mom!" I yell.

"I've got the same problem," she calls from down the hall.

Ellie's door is wide open.

"Guess Dad forgot to hassle you," I say.

"Yeah, lucky me."

We wait for Fred and Bob to come upstairs.

When they see two bedroom doors shut and one open, Brenda's brother shakes his head. "Typical abuser—has to add a little torture to moving day. Wants you to wonder why he hassled you two but not Ellie."

He turns to Mom. "You got one of those skinny metal thingies? The ones that open doors when little kids lock themselves in the bathroom?"

"I think so." She hurries downstairs, returns with one. "Never thought I'd use this again," she says.

Opens our doors like a pro.

Then she gets this funny look on her face. Lifts one finger, says, "Wait. One more thing." She pulls Ellie's door shut and grips the knob. "Stand back everybody." Kicks the door as hard as she can.

WHAM!

Big black smudge gouged into the white paint.

Does it again, then takes off her shoe. Drags the heel back and forth across the door a few times.

What a mess.

I don't know what to say, but Ellie mutters, "Good thing we're moving."

She's right. I'd hate to see Mom trying to match Dad's craziness on a regular basis.

Mom's not worried. She smiles. "Now he can obsess over why someone messed up the *open* door."

I smile back. She's definitely not the same person who left this house.

"I hope he thinks I did it," Ellie says and gives Mom a high five.

Ha! My sister is more like her old self, too.

I'm not. Not with Dad close enough to come in and see Ellie's messed up door. I just want to get through this day. I close my eyes and pray Dad stays outside.

The morning we left home rushes back. We were all so afraid Dad would return and hurt us.

Now it's weeks later. We've been here fifteen minutes, and it looks like I'm the only one who's afraid he'll walk upstairs, see the damage, and go postal.

I want to hide, bad, but I can't go back to being Mike the wuss.

211

I thought I was over that, but Dad is still crazy and we just vandalized his perfectly maintained house. What will he do if he sees Ellie's door? Get us arrested? Sue us?

Then I realize how messed up my thinking is. It's our house, too and it's half Mom's by law! Besides, what's so tough about re-painting *one door* compared to how bad he treated Mom for *years?* How he kept all of us confused, scared, and unhappy?

The times he was nice to me don't count. They were just a plan to get me on his side. The Boys against The Girls.

Only I'm over it. I don't want anything to do with him. I want to live like Master Han when I grow up, not like Dad. I'll find another dojang in the city. Another great Tae Kwon Do teacher.

I don't need Dad's approval to do that. Or anything else.

"Moochie's asleep, the windows are cracked, and the car doors are locked," Brenda calls from the foyer. "What can I do?"

I step into the hall. "Want to assemble boxes?"

"Sure," she says and hurries upstairs. When she sees Ellie's door and Mom standing in front of it holding her shoe, she laughs out loud. "Wow. Way to go, girl!"

Mom nods. "Yeah. About time I let Roberto know he's *done.* The only control he has over me from now on is what I give him, and I'm not giving him *squat.* "

Ellie drags a box into the hall. "Me, neither."

I look in her room. The guys have almost finished taking apart her bed.

Better hustle. My room's probably next.

I grab a box and tackle my closet. Pull out clothes, games, old phones—everything. I can sort stuff out at the apartment. I just want to get out of here.

My soccer ball rolls off the top shelf and I catch it. Its black designs are half worn off, the white parts covered with scuffs. I hold it, feel the memories scratched into its cover. Remember how much fun Dad and I had kicking it around.

And how he'd go inside right after and torture Mom for no good reason.

I carry the ball to their bedroom. Drop it on the bed. Let's see how he likes *my* mind game.

Mom's frantically pulling stuff out of Dad's closet like she's looking for something.

My heart thuds. Oh boy. That's where he always kept Grandpa's shotgun. Suddenly I realize how quiet it's gotten outside.

Where's Dad? Where's the gun?

My brain feels like a cement mixer. Rolls around. Spits out a holiday weekend last year.

We were at the kitchen table finishing lunch. Mom was cooking for a family party at Grandma's. Dad walked over to Mom, started getting friendly.

Ellie and I left the room and turned the TV on. Pretty soon, they started fighting. We turned the sound up loud.

Heard most of it anyway.

"I can't go upstairs with you," Mom said. "I'm running late and I've got to finish the chicken and rice, then shower and change."

Wrong answer. Dad yelled loud enough to break her eardrums, "You think you can deny me my rights, huh? Fine. Maybe I'll 'fix' your car so you can't get to work Tuesday!"

He must have raised his arm to her then, because Mom said, "You hit me and I'll tell the whole family what you do."

Crack.

Probably punched another hole in the wall. Near Mom's head.

The back door slammed hard enough to knock it off its hinges.

We ran to the kitchen. Stood at the stove with Mom, waiting for the truck to roar off.

Breathed easier when it didn't.

"Maybe he's calming down," I said.

Mom said nothing. Turned back to the pot on the stove, fork shaking as she poked the chicken. She was pale, twitchy, hard to read.

I felt like beetles were gnawing at my throat. Dad was still around, and it was always worse when we couldn't see him. When he's lurking.

Fifteen minutes later, he still hadn't come back inside. Hadn't slammed things around on the deck or gone down to his workbench and run the power saw.

"I don't like this," I whispered. "It's different."

Ellie nodded. "Maybe he left her alone because he doesn't want her family to know what he does."

I raised an eyebrow. "Yeah? Maybe Mom should threaten him more often."

Ellie pulled on her hair. "I don't think so."

Mom turned off the burner. "Okay, go get changed, kids. We're leaving in twenty minutes. Don't forget your swim suits and towels."

Ten minutes later, we were back downstairs, pretending to watch a movie on TV. Trying to forget about Dad. He had done stuff like this before other family parties so we knew what would happen. We always ended up going without him, and Mom would make up some story about why he didn't come.

Five minutes later, we heard Mom cry out and a plate crash to the floor.

We ran to the kitchen, stopped dead in the doorway. The first thing we saw was Dad's back.

Then how his left hand was pressing Mom's head against the wall and his right hand was shoving the shotgun into her cheek.

"Robert, stop!" she croaked. "You're hurting me."

I didn't know what to do. Ellie looked around like she was planning to grab something and hit him on the head.

I touched her arm. "Don't!" I whispered. "The gun might go off if you startle him!"

"Gonna make nice now?" Dad sneered.

Mom nodded, tears running down her face.

He lowered the gun and stepped away.

At that moment I hated and feared him more than at any other time in my life. Being stronger than Mom wasn't enough for him anymore. He had used a gun to get his way!

What would he do next, kill her? Kill one of us, if we didn't measure up?

Mom turned off the stove, saw us. Covered the red circle the gun left on her cheek with her hand and followed him upstairs. They passed us silently. She didn't look at us and neither did he.

I wanted to scream. *This is rape, isn't it?*

But I did nothing. Sat down and stared at the TV. Saw nothing.

Wanted to crawl in my closet and hide.

Only I couldn't. I'd hear everything from there.

Today is different. We're not going to be around that long, so Dad won't have a chance to take revenge on Mom or us. And hiding is no option for me. I'm gonna get my stuff, help Mom and the guys, and leave.

I admit I'm still scared of Dad, but I'm stronger than I used to be. I'm living somewhere else and I understand what he's like, what he really cares about. And it's not us.

Which means I've gotta find the freakin' gun and hide it!

I go straight to Dad's closet. Shove the clothes to one side, then shove them the other way. Knock everything off the high shelf and feel all the way to the back. Search every inch of the closet floor and walls.

No gun.

My head pounds, stomach turns to ice. I've got to calm down.

I try to convince myself he sold it or gave it away. But I don't think that's likely. He's desperate now because we're determined to leave him.

What else has he got that can control us as much as a gun?

Mom watches me scour the room. Finally she says, "Forget it. It's not here. I've already looked."

"Maybe we'd better call the police."

"No. That'll set him off for sure. Let's just get out of here as fast as we can."

Maybe she's right. I hope she's right.

"Are the guys taking down your bed?" I ask Mom.

"No, I don't want it."

No surprise there. I return to my room, look out my window at the truck. Don't see Dad, though there's lots of boxes and bags piling up around it.

Señor Asshole, as usual, wants us to wait for his inspection like we're his personal employees. He's hiding to make us scared, to force us to "disobey" him.

Well, screw him!

The guys finish taking my bed apart and carry the mattress out. By the time they've carried the box spring downstairs and I've taken down my posters, my bedroom looks cold as a monk's cell.

Mom hurries past my door, dragging a box of clothes. I grab a couple of my leaf bags and follow her through the garage and outside. Drop them on the grass next to the driveway.

She sighs, looks up at the house. "Okay, let's get the smaller bedroom things."

We carry out lamps, nightstands, pictures, towels and sheets.

Brenda backs Mom's car up so it's near the truck. Moochie whines and barks, but we don't let him out.

We stuff the trunk and fill up part of the back seat. The guys see us doing that and start filling the truck. Mom doesn't stop them. Guess none of us feels compelled to follow Dad's stupid rules.

Soon there are only a few bags left on the front lawn. And still no Dad. We shut the garage door and look at each other.

"Now what?" Mom asks.

I can't believe Dad isn't out here doing his Inspector thing. Looking everything over, arguing over what's his or ours.

"Might as well finish up and leave," Bob says.

Mom nods, so Ellie and I pass three bags to Fred and Bob from the side of the ramp.

"Here's the last two," Mom says, and we cheer.

Ellie looks around. "I hate him, but I wish he'd show his face. This doesn't feel right. It's not Dad's way to let us do what we want."

That's when the front door bangs open, smashes on the wall. Dad steps onto the front stoop, lifts his rifle and points it straight at us.

We freeze, easy targets standing on the driveway a couple yards from a gun.

He steps onto the grass, yells, "I told you I had to see everything before you loaded up!"

Fred and Bob jump off the ramp on our side. Step in front of us and closer to Dad.

He moves further back, his gun feeling like an electric prod though it's ten feet away.

"Okay," he snarls. "You've had your fun. Now you can unload the truck so I can see what you've got!"

"You weren't around," Mom says. "The shelter's already re-assigned our room. We've got to move into the apartment today."

Dad swings the gun toward her. "Shut your trap."

Fred crosses his arms on his chest. "Mr. Castillo, how long you think you can point a gun at us without someone noticing?"

"You shut up, too!" Dad yells. His face is red and his grip on the gun has turned his fingers white. He walks past Fred. Steps sideways so he's facing Mom. The gun is a foot from her stomach. "I said, unload the truck, Mercedes."

She doesn't speak, but she doesn't move, either.

Dad leans forward and lifts the barrel of the gun so it's nearly touching her chest.

"Tough girl, are ya? Don't think I'll pull the trigger, huh?"

He looks like he's a bad actor in an old western movie, only none of us are laughing.

I'm terrified. *What if this isn't just one of his stupid threats? What if the gun is loaded? What if he kills Mom to make his point?*

I inch over until I'm standing next to her. "Dad, you're going too far. Put the gun down, please."

I'm so mad, my voice doesn't shake and I don't want to hide. "Why do you think we left you? Do you think pointing a gun at us will make us want to come home? Do you want to go to jail?"

"I'll put the gun down when you unload the truck."

"We can't do that," I say.

"This is a fifty-fifty state," Mom says. "I'm not breaking the law. I own half the contents of the house, and we didn't take anywhere near that."

"My gun says, 'Prove it!'" Dad yells. He nudges her stomach with the gun barrel.

That's it. There's no use negotiating with a crazy holding a rifle.

I pull out my phone and dial 911. Talk loud when they answer. Tell them our address and what's going on.

I need to make Dad so mad at me, he forgets about Mom. Drops the gun or aims it at me.

"Put that phone away!" he yells and whips the barrel sideways so it's pointed at me.

I don't remember doing this, but Mom says I dropped my phone, set my stance, yelled "Hi-yap!" Lifted my knee and did a perfect side kick.

I remember hearing a crack, like wood breaking. And a scream.

I didn't connect these two sounds with Dad until Bob dragged him to the ground. The gun lay beside them and Dad wasn't even looking at it.

I felt like I was watching a movie. This can't be real. I didn't break my Dad's arm, did I?

Bob lets go and Dad pulls himself up. Sits there, weaving around. Holds his broken arm and stares at the bone poking through his skin.

Mom picks up the gun and points it at Dad. "You didn't win this one, did you Roberto?"

Fred moves behind Dad, ready to grab him if he tries to stand.

I start laughing like a loon. I hurt my father, and he can't hurt me back. He can't hurt anyone! How did I do that?

"Miguel, stop! It's okay," Ellie says. She slaps my shoulder like a girl.

I keep laughing.

Bob grips my shoulders, squeezes hard. "Miguel, calm down! You did good. No one got hurt!"

I stop laughing, start shaking. "We're okay? Mom's okay?"

He nods. "Everyone's okay and she's holding the gun."

"Oh, yeah. Wow."

Police sirens pulse through my head. Two patrol cars fly down our street. Screech to a stop in front of the house.

Four officers jump out. They're wearing vests and helmets. Their guns are pointing at Dad. He raises his head and stares at them like they're from Mars.

Mom drops the gun and crumples to the ground. A female officer picks it up, pumps it. Six shells fall to the ground.

"You bastard," I tell Dad. "You could have killed Mom or me. You had enough shells to kill all of us! Is that what you wanted to do?"

Dad looks at me like he doesn't understand English.

"We got a report you were holding a gun on your wife," the officer says to him. "Why is that?"

Dad shakes his head, sits up straighter but doesn't stand up. "Why do you think, Officer?" he asks. "Look at my arm. My son did this to me! I was protecting myself, protecting my property."

The cop nods her head. "Uh, huh. The 911 dispatcher got two calls. Both callers were sure you were going to kill someone."

A neighbor must have called, too!

Dad looked confused. He really did flip out. Is he crazy for real?

But what would that matter if Mom was dead? I was glad I turned him in. Grateful someone else called, too.

The officer waved over another cop. "Help him up, Joe."

Dad stood there, looking shrunken. Looking like he'd lost the war.

The officer patted him down. "Ok, Mr. Castillo, put your hands together in front."

Dad gasped as the officer cuffed him even though I could tell he was trying to be gentle because of Dad's arm.

"They filled that truck with stuff from my house," he whined. "I caught them sneaking off! I just wanted to scare them. I wasn't gonna do anything."

"No? Then I guess you didn't need a loaded gun."

The other cop read him his rights, pushed him toward a patrol car.

Mom snuck looks at Dad slumped in the car while she answered questions and showed the officers her restraining order.

Ellie was pulling on her hair so hard I couldn't believe it didn't fall out in clumps. "I hope Diego doesn't show up," she says. "That's all we need."

"I don't think he will," I said. "He's smarter than Dad in some ways. Or maybe he's already picked out his next victim."

While the police talk with Brenda and the guys, Mom says, "Let's sit on the grass before I fall down, okay?"

I sit down, put my head on my knees. "I hope Master Han never hears about this."

"Why?" Mom asks.

"Because I hurt Dad so bad."

Ellie looks mad. "So what? You were protecting Mom and us from getting shot. Wouldn't Master Han do that for his family?"

I shrugged. "I don't know. He's so anti-violence."

"Why don't you call him," Mom says. "I know he'd be happy to hear from you."

The last time I called him, he said he missed me, said I was a good student.

I nod. "Yeah, maybe I will."

Several neighbors watch from their sidewalks or yards. I wish I knew who called 911. I think the second call helped, the police got here so fast.

Our neighbors look so shocked and sad. This isn't the kind of neighborhood where men point guns at their family or get pushed into police cruisers.

An officer walks over to us. "You adults need to come down to the station after you finish the move." He looks at Mom. "Will you be coming back here, ma'am?"

She shakes her head. "No. This isn't my home anymore."

The officer nods, takes our new address, and returns to his vehicle.

We wait in the car until Dad and the police leave. The neighbors fade away. I sit there, not knowing how to feel. My father will be in jail. In *jail!* For a long time.

And then I realize that's good and I'm glad because he only cares about himself. He'll never see me again. He can rot in jail or move to the moon. I don't care, as long as he stays away from us.

I'm still buzzing with adrenalin, but my legs and arms feel as if they're made of lead. Feel too heavy for me to stand. Too heavy for me to help with the move.

All I want is for this day to be over so I can climb in bed and sleep for a week.

I look up. Mom is watching the guys close up the truck. I need to stop whining and help out. I squeeze into the back seat of Mom's car, and we follow the truck to the apartment.

We drive in silence. No music, no conversation.

The new neighborhood is mostly brick apartment buildings and two-story houses. Looks nothing like our old one, but has the same Saturday sounds.

I feel better. Dad will be in jail for years, and I don't think he'll get bailed out this time. He won't be able to touch us, threaten us, hurt us anymore.

We unload the truck and the guys set up the beds. My new room is small with a high ceiling. It's also full of boxes. Can't wait to empty them out.

By the time we sit down to lunch, I can even smile at Moochie's excitement and nonstop begging.

Then we hug our friends and helpers goodbye, and Mom follows them to the police station.

I sit on my bed after she leaves, hold my phone. Mom is right. Master Han won't mind if I call him.

I look at the clock. Classes should be over for the day.

He is talking to a parent. Calls me back ten minutes later. "Mike," he says. "Your friend Billy say you move away."

"Yes," I tell him. And I tell him why, tell him what happened today. Tell him what Dad did and what I did.

"I kicked my father and broke his arm." My throat closes up. I can't talk anymore.

He is quiet for a moment. "You did nothing wrong," he says. "You used Tae Kwon Do to save your mother's life, your own life. You are a warrior."

I start crying. A warrior. He said I am a warrior.

"I am proud I was your teacher, proud you use Tae Kwon Do to defend your family."

My breath comes easier. He said it's all right, what I did. I was defending my family and myself.

"Thank you," I whisper. "I plan to find a new *dojang* soon, in the city. I wish it was yours."

"Then work hard for me. And for yourself. Tell me when you are black belt. Maybe someday you teach here."

Without thinking, I bow at his faith in me. Bow as if he's standing in front of me. "I hope I can, Master Han. Thank you."

When we say goodbye, my tears are gone.

The Girls and I are safe. My bedroom walls will be covered with old posters. My clothes will hide the floor and my decrepit sneakers will stink up the closet.

No more inspections. No more warnings.

I'm home.

About the Author

PATRICIA AUST'S LIFE revolved around helping other people. She recognized that for as many children as there were in the battered women's shelter where she volunteered as a children's counselor, there were many more that still were being abused. This book was accepted for publication just before she passed away from cancer on June 12, 2012. Her hope was that this book might help victims of domestic violence to break the cycle.

After she retired from a career in child welfare and specialized foster care, and working for more than 20 years as a public school social worker, she served on various boards of mental health and learning disabilities as well as the Connecticut Task Force on Attention Deficit Hyperactivity Disorder. She belonged to the Society of Children's Book Writers and Illustrators, played in her church's bell choir, and edited *Circuit*, the newsletter of the Learning Disabilities Association of Connecticut. What she loved most, though, was writing middle-grade and young adult novels.

For Every
Individual...

Renew by Phone
269-5222

Renew on the Web
www.indypl.org

For General Library Information
please call 275-4100